Happy Days of the GRUMP

First published in Finland in as Ilosia Aikoja,
Mielensäpahoittaja in 2010 by Werner Söderström

First published in Great Britain in 2017 by Manilla Publishing,
80–81 Wimpole St, London, W1G 9RE
www.manillabooks.com

A CIP catalogue record for this book is available from the British Library.

ISBN: 978-1-78658-026-9

Also available as an ebook

This book was produced by IDSUK (Data Connection) Ltd

Manilla Publishing is an imprint of Bonnier Zaffre,
a Bonnier Publishing company
www.bonnierzaffre.co.uk
www.bonnierpublishing.co.uk

TUOMAS KYRÖ

Happy Days of the Grump

of the

GRUMP

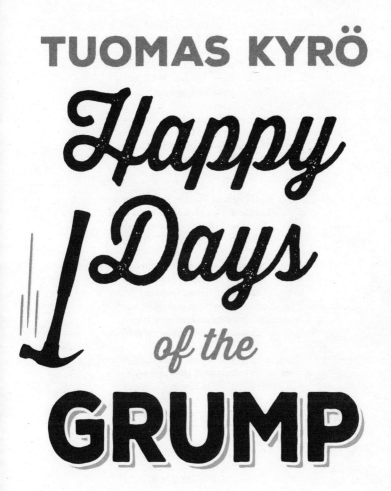

MANILLA

Like an oak

Well, it sure ruined my day when life emptied my
workshop all over the floor. I was looking in my tool
cupboard for a medium-sized chisel so that I could
finish off what I was making, but instead I pulled out
a cardboard box. Loose photographs and a fragile
album toppled to the floor. I piled up the loose pictures,
put them back into the box and lifted it on to the
work-bench.

I had decided that it's pointless to look at old
pictures; I remember what I remember of this life. I put
the important pictures on my wall, the ones of people
I admire – there are two of them; an Olympic gold
medal-winning javelin throwers and a news anchor.
That's enough for me. Anything else is superfluous and
can stay in the cardboard boxes or bureau drawers.

But I had to take a little peek in the album.

On the inside pages I found my father's name, written in fountain pen, and the date 1913, and all of a sudden I remembered looking through the album's six pictures as a little boy with my mother in one of the brief moments when there was no work to do between tanning leather and cleaning fish. Between someone being born and someone dying. I also remembered my father wondering what kind of a job being a photographer really involved. At the bottom of each photograph was the legend *Photographer K.R. Åkström* and what I knew about him was that he spoke a strange kind of Finnish and, in addition to photographic equipment, sold little bottles of spirits during the years when alcohol was nowhere to be found.

In the first photograph in the album, my father and my mother stand side by side, newly engaged, although they looked as if they had been photographed for the state police archive. Behind the smiles they looked scared. It sure wasn't easy in those days to get married or to pose for the camera.

Then came a picture with me in it, in my mother's lap. Twenty-five-year-olds in those days looked different from today. My mother wore a scarf on her head and clothes almost as heavy and drab as life itself. In addition to me, there was an older child – how could I have forgotten him? Urpo, the neighbours' orphaned child was living with us until he was old enough to work. In the picture, Urpo looked like a miniature adult, although he would have been six years old at most. Next to us is a sapling a little shorter than orphan Urpo, planted by my father the day I was born. The oak still grows today in my garden, so big that my son Hessu, Dr Kivinkinen, and the social worker all think it should be felled at once. They are scared it may fall on to the house. But it won't fall until I cut it down and even if it did, a good house couldn't have a better ending.

The last full picture in my parents' album was of a completely unfamiliar person sitting in the back of someone's horse-drawn cart. I sure couldn't say whether it was a week day, a festival or a funeral.

The very last picture was a half-picture.

It was a picture of a man and a woman, holding each other's hands. The photograph had been torn so that the faces were missing, and in the bottom right-hand corner was a stain.

There was another flash in my memory.

My father had brought the picture back from the war and the stain was blood. I sure don't know what a photograph like that was doing in our family album. It really is better that nowadays you can make friends from other countries by exchanging letters, not bullets.

Beside the loose photographs I found an envelope marked 'Important'. Inside was an entry ticket for the Salpausselkä games, a Middle Finland–Kajaani timetable, but best of all, the newspaper cutting with my father's mother's death notice and my father's fiftieth birthday announcement next to it. There was only a week between the two events and my father had taken the notices to the newspaper office at the same day, thinking he might get a discount for placing the two orders at the same time. In fact, all that happened was that the two texts changed places.

Granny's death notice read: I WILL NOT BE CELEBRATING.

Father's birthday announcement read: Blessed are the pure in heart, for they will see God (Matt. 5:8).

I closed the envelope, put the album into the dresser drawer and began to go through the loose photographs. Pictures from different dates were randomly mixed together, black-and-white and colour, large and small, school photos and passport photos. I looked at my wife as a young girl, before we met. She was smiling in her summer clothes, just as I always remember her. Light and feminine, even when she was tormented by the mosquitoes in the cloudberry bogs or by the varicose veins in her legs.

Now, as I looked at the old photographs, I felt as if I had stepped into them. I sure was amazed when I suddenly remembered the itchiness of woollen socks against bare skin, and the feel of my wife's hip when my hand touched her while a family photograph was being taken.

The fog disappeared before my eyes. The present day disappeared. I wasn't looking at the photographs from today, but from when they were taken.

At this age, long years and slow events are like flashes of lightning. You can't take anything with you, and nothing much of yourself remains here. That's why you should be able to go exactly as you wish, and who else knows what I want?

The telephone brought me back to reality. It was half-past seven, the time when my son rings. Every morning at the same time he checks that I am OK, what I have done, what I'm going to do. I pressed the green button on my phone and announced that I had been going through the lives of my parents and of myself. I knew what I had to do today, and I would do it quickly. I had to go to the care home, the fabric shop, the hardware store and to buy some ink.

Bring the horses in!

I showed my wife our wedding photograph and remembered how I'd wanted to go straight home from the church. I'd wanted to tear the tight collar from my neck, put on my boots and grab my spade. What's the use of just standing there shaking hands with people and eating cake? My wife smiled a bit and I felt that this was the kind of day when she might understand what I said.

I remembered out loud how my wife threatened that our marriage would be a short one unless I agreed to the wedding waltz. I had to be fetched from sulking in the attic. That's the one and only time I've danced and hopefully there are no photographs from that occasion.

I waited for the food to cool. I lifted up the photographs for my wife to see them – sometimes she smiled, sometimes she turned her eyes to meet mine. I asked whether life really had been as it appeared in the photographs or whether it was just the moment or the way people were posed. In a realistic picture my mother would be in the kitchen, my father in the logging forest and I would be taking hay to the horses, but how can you take a picture in three places at the same time? I suppose the sun shone then, too – the world can't have been black and white? Perhaps fresh pike-perch was being grilled and someone had an accordion.

My wife moved her head a bit and I thought it looked like a nod. I tried the food with my little finger and gave her the first spoonful. I told my wife that you never have pictures of the moments you want, for example when I dared for the first time to jump head-first off the cliffs at Lake Porsajärvi. Another example would be a series of pictures of my wife, and they would go like this: she would lean out of the window as I came home from work. I would wave to her and she'd wave back and call out to tell me that dinner was on the table, which of course I knew from the smell of the potatoes.

I also had in my pocket three letters my wife had written to me, which I found in the box of photographs. I kept them with me even though I did not want to read them.

'I'm not eating, I'm not hungry, and the horses still need tending,' came a voice from the next bed.

I put the photographs in the plastic folder and concentrated on feeding my wife.

'If you won't eat, Anneli dear, I will have to feed you,' said the carer.

She dipped some rye bread in milk and tried to coax Anneli to open her mouth. More food ended up on the floor than inside her. There must be a reason why my wife likes her food and Anneli doesn't. Maybe it's our own potatoes and the smoked pork that I mix with the hospital food.

'Why's she getting better stuff?' Anneli asked. 'Why aren't I getting any of that neck of pork?'

I told the nurse that the strange smell of smoked meat must be coming from the air-conditioning vents. I wasn't going to get caught with my own potatoes, because I well know how hospitals scrutinise minerals, salts and sugars. Nutritional values are more important than good taste and the happiness that tasty food brings.

When you're in life's final furlong, you shouldn't have to eat the same as at the beginning, in nurseries and primary schools. It's sensible to be careful with what children eat, because in working life they will end up glued to their ergonomically designed chairs in warm offices, and in jobs like that you need completely different chow from my generation. Human beings are strange creatures because our bodies have not kept up with our minds.

My aches and pains came from the fact that I have used the same bones and muscles to do outside work from the age of four. Today's youth go outside for the first time when they are ten, because the weather's always either too cold, too hot, too windy or too settled.

So my wife sure has every right to her smoked pork and her knob of butter, and Anneli should have the same right, too.

My wife tasted the second spoonful between her lips as little children sample unfamiliar foods. Trying to work out whether it was treat or poison. She swallowed and opened her mouth again like a baby bird. I offered her the next spoonful and told her how the photographs had cheered me up. There are still a few things I haven't done in my life.

'Are you making a Wendy house for your grand-children?' the nurse asked.

I told her I had made one of those years ago, in the Fifties. Now it was time to make something just for myself.

Gradually, my wife began to enjoy her food. That's what happens if you are patient, if you remember to live at my wife's pace and not your own, that you're hurrying because it's nearly time for the news. If you hurry, her mouth clamps shut or the porridge you've just spooned in comes right back out. At the same time Anneli in the next bed closed her mouth with an imaginary zip.

'Oh my goodness,' the nurse said. 'I have to finish my round. I'll come back at the end and hope that Anneli will be more willing to co-operate.'

When the nurse had gone, Anneli whispered to me that she had to get out of here. She intended to take with her the pieces of bread she had left uneaten, and she had stockpiled a fistful of sugar lumps inside a pillowcase, plus the same amount of salt. Anneli said she knew where the main door was; if she picked the right moment she would be able to use it to escape. I understood her desire very well. No one's comfortable behind locked doors, at least if they realise they are behind locked doors. Often old men and old women waited beside the ward door in case it was left ajar, and if someone left it open, a search for the old men and old women was mounted, with official bulletins and volunteer helpers. I tried to convince Anneli that we were safe. She looked me in the eyes for a moment as if she'd understood something important.

'Bring the horses in!' Anneli cried.

I said I didn't think there were any horses here.

Anneli tried to get up, but it was a long time before she remembered which foot she should put on the floor first. My wife didn't like loud noises, and she began to moan a little.

'What's the matter here?' asked the nurse, who had returned to the room with a mother's anxiety. She looked at me, too, as if I were Anneli's companion in crime. I said that we were bringing the horses in and going to Viipuri.

'Anneli, sit down!' the nurse said. 'Calm down. Eat.'

Giving orders really doesn't help calm a person down. First one person shouts, then the other shouts back not to shout. And then a third person arrives and demands why the hell are you shouting, do you need a whack in the gob. If a child is shouting you should put a nail in one hand and a hammer in the other. Or a hot potato. Perhaps a book, if they're a reader. Something to do is what they need.

My wife's eating ended there and then.

I cooled the coffee for a moment by stirring it. My wife slurped three times from the beaker and began to get ready to go to sleep. I brushed her hair back from her forehead, gave her an extra quilt and lowered the bed into its sleeping position. I turned out the light. Outside, it was mid afternoon. The street lights were coming on; the sky was turning from twilight to darkness. I twisted the venetian blinds shut. My wife was already asleep.

Anneli looked at the nurse, a taut wrinkle between her eyes, and the nurse didn't really know what to do.

'Felt boots, good felt boots! The old man took the cap! Bring the horses in!'

I said that the horses were absolutely fine, I said I had got them to follow me here by bringing my own packed lunch. I took the packet of smoked pork from my pocket and let Anneli use her own fingers to swipe a slice, two, three. She smacked her lips and said she often eats things like this when she goes to town with the old ladies. Anneli asked if there was any mackerel. She suspected that you could only get food this good on the black market, and I didn't deny it. Anneli asked if there had been any bombing during the night, and whether the horses had stayed calm.

I looked for an old baby picture among the photographs. I gave it to Anneli and said that it should be well cared for; it was only a couple of months old. Anneli nursed the picture and looked at the child. She chatted to it in a low voice; I nodded and said that's good, and the crying stopped at once. I said the cap and the felt boots were drying on top of the stove. I promised to take some hay to the horses when I left. Then I put the dishes on the tray, turned out the lights and took the tray to the kitchen.

I sat down for a moment in the TV room. Leafing through today's paper, in which things were even more awry than they'd been two days earlier. Insanities had been happening in finance, because money is no longer notes but merely numbers in the computer networks of the Central Bank. From there it is lent, invested, stolen, twisted and turned beyond recognition – money that has never even existed. Then the computer network reveals debts and receipts for which subsidies and stimulus packages had to be created. Really, potatoes would have been easier to trade in. If someone could work out a way to package potatoes and sense in the same sack and how to pack those sacks into a container, export trade would definitely increase.

Into the TV room tiptoed Risto Lipponen, who had once been the most important tax-payer in the village. He traded in cars and electronics and built two blocks of flats whose reinforced concrete I was involved in making. Prosperity was visible in Risto's expensive brick-built house, his German cars, which got bigger every year, and his similarly swollen belly.

He retired and I retired, and I did not see Risto Lipponen for fifteen years until he sat himself down in the rocking chair at this moment, a piss stain on his trousers. Not for Risto the retirement days on the golf courses of Spain that he announced in his birthday interview. He also claimed that he had always been an entirely sober and honest man.

That's life. You can't do anything about it.

I am sure a medicine for memory diseases will be invented. There are cures for polio and tuberculosis and AIDS. But it only means that a moment later nature comes back with an even more mischievous form of flu. Risto Lipponen stared at me for a long time while I tried to maintain a slightly distant and briskly amicable expression.

'Guess how long I've been here?' Risto Lipponen asked.

I guessed as long as the section C of the newspaper.
'Try again.'

A one-column news story?

'Wrong again. You've not got a lot of sense, have you? Shall I answer, since you can't?'

I nodded. Risto Lipponen counted his fingers for a long time, as children do.

'An eternity is how long I've been here.'

I asked if Risto's eternity would be helped by some smoked pork and mashed potato.

'I'd prefer some of my favourite drink,' Risto whispered.

I sure wouldn't want Risto's fate for myself, or Anneli's. A person has to have a plan in the event of brain diseases and other threats. If I lose my reason and end up wandering around like an idiot, then the direction is clear. The cloudberry bog. Or the shore of the Arctic Sea. I will forget where I am, and disappear into a quarry. Then the newspapers are welcome to report that an old man was found in the swamp, stiff with cold, as long as they remember to say that his buckets were full of cloudberries and his boots well polished.

I look after my wife. Who will look after me? Will my son come and feed me? I have my doubts. Will I want him to come? Certainly not. Will it be the nurse who turns me over in bed, sees my backside and my front, who gives me a shower, thinking her own thoughts, like what she needs to buy from the shop, does the cat have food, reflecting, goodness this gentleman smells of a lived life?

Why live your last years at the mercy of others, when you've always been so independent – when as early as five you knew how to make porridge, milk a cow, untangle a net and dig a ditch? And what if I suddenly find myself in a completely different time? The time when I have only seen seventeen summers, buying motor parts? I drive through villages and claim I own places. I eat Saturday sausage on the churchyard bench and forget to wear my long-johns.

I won't agree to nappies. Neither will tubes or infusion bags have any contact with my body or skiers' bodies for that matter. I must express my wishes while I still can. It is equitable, economically sustainable and environmentally friendly.

My wife thought about these things differently, because wives think differently. For them, caring and being cared for are easier. They want to be held by the shoulders, massaged and comforted. They know how to return the favour. It is not difficult for them to ask for help or to accept a hug. Even in her bed, she looks as if she would rather be in this world than not. Every day I look into her eyes. Every day they fade a little, but they have not gone out.

If there is no one who remembers me as I was, do I exist? Who knows who Anneli used to be? Are there photographs left, any writing? Do we know anything about the years when she, along with Risto Lipponen, was full of life and strength?

Do they?

One.way.or.another.

I was in a fabric shop for the first time in my life and I knew what I wanted. But blow me if there wasn't a shop assistant at my back asking how could she help me, as if she really had any interest in anything but the notes in my wallet. I am more than suspicious of shops with warm, carefully considered lighting in which assistants give warm, carefully considered advice about whether this will go with your floor, window or wedding dress.

It sure is better not to reveal anything about your plans to strangers, but you have to say something so that they don't think you're a shoplifter. The easiest thing is to talk about the weather, although it was velvet I wanted, and that's what my wife would have wanted, too.

I told the shop assistant that this morning had been the warmest for thirteen years and the ground was still green. Normally at this time of year you would be able to go skiing; now there was no snow anywhere. The assistant nodded and pulled out a bolt of too-bright red cloth. I told her how flies had been buzzing between the window panes; they must have thought it was spring although it's actually December. Those innocent creatures don't understand what's good for them and for that reason I haven't bothered to swat them; let them buzz away on the pastries if it makes them happy.

'This is the fashionable colour of the moment, or, erm, maybe that one over there . . . Might you consider . . .'

I put the fabric suggested by the assistant back in its place and took out a calm green, which in another light looked black. And a suitable amount of lace edging. The assistant cut the fabrics to length and I checked the measuring rod to see that she wasn't cheating me. When we moved over to the till, I asked for a handful of white- and red-headed drawing pins. For free.

'Errm, I'm really not allowed to give preferential treatment, sir. We have offers across the whole chain for everyone's benefit, if you know what I mean.'

It's not preferential treatment, but cultivating customer relations. Things like this get more expensive for me, and cheaper for the shop, year by year. That, of course, is something young people don't understand – nor does the American shareholder whose desires, needs and fancies dictate what you can do in Finland's fabric or tyre shops. All I'm asking for is justice and fairness, which at this moment would be a handful of white and red drawing pins.

The assistant narrowed her gaze; she had clearly never been confronted by such complex decisions in all her nineteen years.

'Oh well, OK,' the assistant said. 'But you won't . . . you won't tell anyone. You know. Like.'

Who would I tell? I asked, as I put the drawing pins in a bag and the bag in my coat pocket. In the old days I could have told Yrjänä, but how do you make contact with the dead? Yrjänä would have known how to talk about such things and remember friends we had in common and fabric shops from days gone by. He was a talker where I preferred to remain silent. My wife knew how to buy fabrics, cups and birthday cards. I know how to buy a hoe and a car, an Escort.

I crossed the road to the hardware store. Or of course it's no longer a hardware store, but an interiors and building supplies merchant. They always have to play with words and make things difficult. When you've got a good, clear word like cleaner, then it's always changed to something like hygiene and cleanliness worker. Soon people won't be people, but organisms capable of communication, according to their skills and desires, whose prime asset is the opposable thumb.

In the hardware store I was able to find my way around and stand my ground. I knew where the paint was, and what paint I needed. But here, too, there was an enthusiastic sales assistant to be avoided. When he made towards me I ducked from the paint section to the tool section and from the tool section to the tile section. Sales assistant school clearly misses out the course about pushiness driving away lots of good customers.

I took a tin of white gloss paint, a tin of stain lacquer and some acetone, and three rolls of masking tape. I went to the till, where the owner himself was on duty. He was a shopkeeper of the third generation and had the worst voice in the church choir, but he was clever. Today, too, he immediately threw in a paintbrush and remarked that the weather was reasonable.

Shopkeepers are complicated, if you think about it. They pay the highest rates in tax, providing plenty of rulers for the primary schools and blood-test needles to the health centre. They're also able to skate around excessive taxes. Shift subcontracting businesses and subsidiaries to Estonia. Vote for the Progressive Party and invite each other to big parties on Independence Day.

The clever shopkeeper does not flaunt his money. The hardware store owner lives in the same house as he did in the Sixties and does not boast by renovating the façade. Inside, his house may be made of diamonds and swimming pools, but of course I don't see that. He understands the virtue of driving an ordinary car and has not upgraded to an Audi even though he must be tempted to spend the income that's announced in the local paper once a year.

For a shopkeeper, everyone's a customer, and he's a shopkeeper for everyone. A good shopkeeper is not arrogant; he values a little boy's pile of coins just as much as the credit card of someone who's building a house. The boy who buys sweets will one day be a house-builder.

I wished the shopkeeper a good day. The shopkeeper said something about skiing conditions and you could see that he knew his customer. Then he nodded and looked me in the eye as if he really was my friend. As I approached the door, I turned back to look and saw the shopkeeper already becoming best mates with the next customer.

I walked from the hardware store to the grocer's shop.

I bought buttermilk, and some overpriced lactose-free milk for my son. You have to know how to promote your own products, but the best selling point is that the things you're selling really are quality goods. Then they can be expensive, too. After this morning's conversation my son would probably rush round to see how I was. It was his habit nowadays; he came without announcement, tidying places that were already clean, asking the sort of thing you ask old people and insisting on making food for the freezer. He always used the electric hob because he'd never learned to use the oven. He thought it was slow, although it was he who was slow. In the hundred-metres race in Year Five he took more than fifteen seconds.

I let him come because it's important to him. And it's better to have my son to look at than my own reflection in the kitchen window. He could bring the children more often, but they have horse-riding, chemistry tests, friends' birthday parties, a violin concert or just need to catch up on sleep. Anyway, my son is probably in touch with the council health and old people's services and together they will be working on a care plan for me. My life is being organised by people whose parents I helped carry to the grave and whose goings-on I have been following from the snotty-nose phase to the eye make-up phase, the moped-riding phase and the cool youth phase. It sure ruins my day when one of them shouts *how are we today, can you still manage on your own, do you still drink coffee, can you still hold a cup, have you had stair-rails installed?*

I took a bus home, sitting two rows behind the driver, next to the window. We fetched the school-run children, of whom there is now only one since the family from the blue house moved to a bigger village. The boy asked me what I had in my bags. I showed him the fabrics and the paints; the boy wondered if I was going to build a completely new room in the old house, just like they do on the television programmes his mother watched. I told him I was making a coffin.

Khomeini or Kekkonen?

You shouldn't make a coffin. According to my son,
I should just sit on a sofa goggling at German cops
'n' robbers series on the TV. If I'm allowed to build
something, then it should be a bird-box or wall-clock.
I told him I already had a clock in every room, two in
my bedroom. A person who tells you to build more
bird-boxes is a birdbrain.

'You seemed a bit cryptic on the phone.'

With my son, I often find myself having to speak a
completely different kind of Finnish to the one I know.

'I was worried you might have some kind of blood
pressure problem. Do you think so? Do you find
yourself losing your balance or going sort of dizzy?'

I felled the trees for the coffin many Olympics ago,
dried them first in the cowshed porch, then let them

rest in the attic for a moment, for thirteen years. Half
pine, half birch. It's important what season you fell
them in, so that the timber will curve in the way you
want it to. My own coffin I will not paint or plane or
lacquer. On top of the velvet will go my day quilt, the
brown and yellow one, on which my wife embroidered
my initials. It's terribly ugly, but so soft and warm.
For my wife I plane and lacquer and decorate. I make
wooden lace with a chisel. White, it needs to be. My
wife will get what she would want. For other people
you need to make what's good for them, even if they
don't understand it.

'Wooden lace? What are you talking about, Dad?
What is it you don't think we understand?'

A coffin sure isn't anything more than a vessel for
transporting a person. It's silly for the heirs to use their
money on anything like that. If you're careful to save
money when you're buying a car, a bicycle or a cart, then
why waste it when it comes to a coffin? It is on show
for just one day; you never have to service it or buy it
hubcaps.

The coffin shop man is after the last penny from the
mourners, and you can avoid that if you are prepared.
People are lowered to their final rest in finest suits,
even if they were more comfortable in sweatpants
or overalls while they were alive. In the church hall,
a lot of nonsense is said about the fine citizen and
benefactor whom the minister didn't really know at all.
Of course, a few people really will be grieving, but the

rest want to get to the oxtail soup as soon as they can and are worrying about whether they look sufficiently mournful, whether they are drooling, whether they can summon a sympathetic smile to their lips from time to time. Or then they're in a hurry to feed the cows. Or to watch the first trials for the fifteen hundred metres.

Then there is the group of haters, who are fed up to the back teeth with all the fine words when they remember well how mean and selfish the dead person really was. For example, the man who didn't bother to return the circular saw he borrowed – now doesn't seem quite the right moment to ask the heirs for it back. But why not? It was a good circular saw, with the original blade. Like the one I lent to Kolehmainen. Why did I do that? He's still alive, of course, but I haven't got round to raising the subject. I could raise it with his wife, she is a Thai berry-picker, a fine person, but we lack a common language. It's certain that the circular saw will not return to my descendants; instead, Kolehmainen will sell it through the small ads columns and claim it's in good condition for its age, throwing in some useless object like a fan that he's bought on his travels in the Far East.

'Dad, seriously,' my son said. 'Funeral expenses just aren't a problem, or the saw, and especially not Kolehmainen. The problem is the fact that no one has died. There's no need to be making a coffin for anybody.'

What has death got to do with making a coffin, anyway? As many people leave here as arrive. Coffins are needed just as much as potatoes or dentists. The funeral trade has always been a more secure way of earning your bread-and-butter than the research into developing countries which my son studied for seventeen-odd years.

'I, errm, changed my main subject,' he'd admitted. 'I began to feel somehow closer to women's studies. You know, it's currently a really essential aspect of the problematic of modern society . . .'

The funeral trade is a growth area for the future. My generation was content with simplicity, but it will be different in the year 2050. Even in the coffin, there will have to be constant loud music, central heating, air conditioning, cushions and a fridge. And fifty per cent more timber will be needed for one person's coffin because people are constantly getting fatter and exercising less. Cardboard factories, too, are doing well because the beard-and-sandals brigade want to go to their graves in a modest and eco-friendly way.

My son insisted that my wife was still lying in the health centre ward and that Kivinkinen had prophesied 107 years of life for me; 109 if I would just agree to swap full-fat milk for fat-free.

I withdrew a bit, because I understood what was at stake here.

My son was afraid.

He was afraid of where it inevitably ends, this human journey. In the fact that we have to take responsibility for our demise.

'Why don't I go and make some coffee. Isn't it coffee time, for you, I mean – I don't drink it, as you know. So, tea instead . . . Do you have any tea, Dad?'

Yes, I do have the packet I bought for him in 'Ninety-eight.

I asked him to pass me the plane before he left. He gave me the file. What's the matter with him, why can't he tell the difference, at his age? Looks as if a file is an unnecessary object for his generation, apart from my daughter-in-law's nail file.

I took a step back and considered what I had achieved. It looked good and straight, with enough room for the shoulders.

A day came into my mind – the day when my old man and I listened to Stalin's funeral on the radio. On the table was a layer cake, and we didn't often have one of those. I sure didn't feel like eating it. Even though Mr Moustache was a terrible ruler who moved his people around and changed the directions of rivers when he was drunk and was a terrible brawler. I can't eat cake when someone dies. Dad took four extra pieces and went back to the larder in the evening too.

That was certainly enough for one day.

I don't have energy to do much any more. An hour is enough unless something's urgent. It's best to finish when you have the appetite and strength for the following day. I switched off the light and pulled the door shut.

Inside, I sat down at my kitchen table and put my palms flat on the table. I asked my son to pull the

splinters from under my nails, since it's beginning
to be hard for me to peer so close. I can see and
remember far away best: you can imagine distant things
accurately, just as you'd actually see them.

'Can you wait a minute, I'll just watch this to the
end?' my son replied in the same way he'd spoken ever
since he was a child. It's what young people do, they
think the television is like Uncle Veijo, whose talk never
ends and never becomes interesting but you have to
watch programmes to the end.

I asked again, and slowly my son began to get up
from the sofa. He used his balance and his centre of
gravity quite wrongly; if you get up that way you're
bound to have back problems and an early retirement.

I showed him the longest splinter, which my son
grasped timidly. He looked me in the eye, asking if he
dared pull it, and I chivvied him to do something. Blood
was oozing from under the nail, and funerals other
than Stalin's began to come to mind. At the end of the
Eighties, in Persia, the bearded man and demagogue
Khomeini was carried to his grave. In Persia men have
dresses and many metres of fabric wound around their
heads. A dress would be pleasantly cool, since you don't
have to wear anything under it and the wind goes from
one sleeve to the other. Why don't men wear clothes like
that here? If I were to put on a dress, there would soon
be a white van and flashing lights outside the house, or a
current affairs journalist who would ask me what it was
like to be a modern man. Khomeini sure wouldn't have
placed a high value on home-made trousers.

Khomeini's life may be harder than an ordinary person's life, because he is responsible for a whole nation and also has to wage war against a superpower. There's a lot of noise made about religion, as if life were nothing more than a revivalist meeting. It's not, it's ordinary. Someone like Khomeini would never be able just to go down to the lake to lift his fish traps.

There were so many people at the memorial service that it was bedlam.

'Does it hurt a lot?'

Khomeini was already dead, why on earth was he asking? It was probably a relief.

'Taking out your splinters. Does it hurt?'

No more than taking off your shoes.

I wonder what they offer funeral guests in Persian church halls. Is it the Persian venison Karelian stew, this kebab, which you can buy even here in our village from the shop where the insulation store used to be? Or was it the bus station? Anyway, now Anatolu Kebab is there and I have tasted them on at least two occasions. Not bad, even though they use funny flavourings, such as allspice. Then there's a kind of liquid on top of it all, which is good enough to eat more of, except that it makes you go to the loo. I'm sure Persia has its own Karelian stew; everywhere does.

'Well, I haven't studied the festival or food traditions of the Near East in any depth,' said my son.

I guessed that in addition to the kebab there would be some kind of cabbage salad, a thin, warm flatbread without butter and, to drink, a goats' yoghurt drink.

Of course the young people and youths of the Near East would like to replace these with sweet carbonated drinks and electric guitar music, and nothing that had any meaning for their own parents and grandparents has any meaning any more.

I made a coffee and sat in the rocking chair. I ask whether my son remembered the funeral of our own country's Khomeini, President Kekkonen. Both of them blokes you can't get rid of even after they die. In life they had too much power and after death half the people yearn for a strong leader. The other half climb out of the bunkers to say how awful it was down there, and they go on about it for a generation. The bad times are blamed on Khomeini, Kekkonen or a councillor.

'Did you watch it on TV?' my son asked. 'With Mum? Did you drink coffee and watch them on TV? I kinda remember that I might have watched too.'

We sure didn't watch it on TV, or drink coffee. We had better things to do; we had to empty the manure silo. I still maintain that a home-made coffin and generally less fuss would have been fine for either Khomeini or Kekkonen, maybe even one of those cardboard coffins. There was no need to parade them around town or walk behind black limousines.

Since sure else came to mind, I made an attempt to lighten the atmosphere a little. I wondered what cremation would be like. I've seen a documentary about how the dead are cared for at other latitudes and in other cultures. At high temperatures it sure is sensible to destroy flesh and bones at once, but what I don't know is whether the Indians know how to use embers properly. Do they use the fire for a robber's roast to eat afterwards? Do they use the residual heat for industrial purposes? Do they tell campfire tales? Burning bodies on a bonfire would make sense in Finland, too.

'Why not?' my son smiled briefly, but then took it back. 'We shouldn't laugh at things like that. Not, like, at my age, anyway. At your age it's different. I mean, an experience like that . . . or maybe it's the point of view.'

I wasn't laughing at anything, just thinking about how things could be organised more effectively. It's hard to get bone to burn so it would be worth collecting the bones and giving them to children as toys. They could fence with thigh bones or use skulls in dramatic productions. That's what people do today, after all. They always have to be on show.

'I sure don't think the hygiene officials would agree . . .'

Of course there are things where permission should be asked, like suttee and wars of aggression, but why shouldn't you be allowed to choose your own final resting place? While you're alive, after all, you're allowed to torture your body with alcohol, tobacco, earrings, general idling and messing around. Why is it that something that has during life been a general rubbish dump should become sacred after death? My son set the plates on the table and asked me to sit down. The vegetables for the soup had been cut completely wrong, into weird strips. I said nothing and ate.

Between the first and second bowlfuls I remembered one more funeral.

Tauno Pokkinen met the end of his road in the spring of 'Sixty-six. He fell through the ice while he was fishing. He didn't die there and then, but on the journey home, on a bend, when he insisted on proving that even a man numb with cold can turn the wheel. But he couldn't turn it, and Tauno crashed into a tree. Anyway, Tauno was a young man then, because I was still quite young. We weren't friends, but from time to time, when doing volunteer work, we would drink juice from the same bottle and eat sausages.

I sat in the back row of the church and looked at old Pokkinen and old Mrs Pokkinen. It was as if they were carved from stone. It was no use the women hugging and the men trying to look them in the eye and at the ceiling at the same time. Parents sure shouldn't have to go to their children's funerals. It turns the world upside down.

'Couldn't we change the subject?'

Of course we could change the subject. It was time to talk about my will.

An archive for beam-carvers?

You make your last will on good paper, with your dead father's fountain pen which he inherited from his own father. With the same pen he used to write his own name on the first page of the photograph album. In addition to the pen, father inherited a stony parcel of land across which the council drove a paved road. There was nothing to be done, even though we appealed in writing and to the village committee on the grounds of emotional traumas sustained, impairment to livelihood, loss of profits and harm to all sorts of protected animal species. This happened in 'Eighty-three. Twenty years went by and a bigger paved road was put through a couple of kilometres from the first one, because you always need to design the next car to be faster than the one before and roads have to keep up.

I understand how footpaths or carriageways are made where once was just forest, bog and rocky ground, not to mention hostile tribes. A road, as well as peace between the tribes, is essential. Trade begins, new wives and husbands are found on the other side of the lake or sea. Blood mixes, people begin to see more clearly. That kind of development is important.

'I can't hear you,' said my son, who was waist-deep in the upper closet. 'Is it this orange box?'

It sure wasn't. It was packed full of old *Seura* magazines waiting for them to become valuable. I told him to look for a box labelled 'Chiquita' like the banana and within it a smaller packet labelled 'Pelikan'.

My son passed me a portable typewriter and a bag of odd socks and a bundle of old bills. Finally he found what we were looking for and passed the box to me. I opened it carefully and there it was, the nib intact and a small bottle of ink beside it.

I told him that the pen had been used once, forty years earlier, when we took out the first and last loan of our lives. For three years I had taken my pay packet straight to the bank manager and never drank coffee even if it was offered in a porcelain cup. In a loan arrangement you should never let someone else, the National Share Bank or your father, get one over you. You need to discharge your obligations; you can be fishing buddies later.

Porridge, potatoes and crispbread were what we ate during our debt years. My son says he remembers it well, but according to him we also ate porridge, potatoes and crispbread after the years I referred to. I certainly remember, after the last payment, buying a big loop of the better sausage and putting two sugars in my coffee. Cream biscuits for the children, sugar and cream in our own cups. I asked if he remembered that, remembered how we'd celebrated.

'Well maybe yes . . . a kind of . . . atmosphere . . . now you mention it. Can I have a look, it's a fine pen?'

According to my wife we should have taken out a bigger loan. She wanted radiators in the house. I thought that kind of notion pure madness, but my wife kept on asking the question for many days. She had heard from her sisters that in the city houses were heated by district heating – you no longer had to carry the logs in. Even the loo worked by pulling a chain, and the pan never had to be emptied.

And that's where it went wrong, this whole world. The forests are full of timber, houses have fine fireplaces, but why on earth is it necessary to ship oil from Khomeini's war zones or natural gas from beneath the Siberian permafrost and give Russia's tiny dictator power to blackmail countries smaller than his? It sure would be better the other way around. The Finns and the Canadians should export timber to the big-arsed men of Arabia and America, who can't even visit the fridge without getting in their cars.

My wife didn't like what I said. We had an argument about it, a big argument. I wasn't going to tell my son about it now.

The lid of the ink bottle was tight.

I needed to use pliers.

'If you have to make your will, why don't you do it on the computer?'

Let's keep knowledge and machines separate.

'We could print one of those ready-made layouts off the internet. I could do it at home and post it to you, couldn't I?'

I sure don't trust computers; the pen is a fine invention, after all. How would my will survive on the computer all the way back to my son's home? What if a virus attacked the computer on the way, or bird flu my son?

'I'll make a back-up copy. I'll save it on to a memory stick and onto The Cloud as well, if you like.'

Well, sure, in the old days you recorded important information on paper and then put it in a bank vault. Maybe you'd take a carbon copy, which would be put in another store. Now all the information, photographs, journals and bank statements can fit onto something which the human eye cannot see. Young people watch old television series on their phones and listen to yeah-yeah music whenever they want to.

This is what it is: wrong.

The young lads no longer remember the difference between special and ordinary time. It's computers that are to blame.

I couldn't get the ink bottle open even with the pliers. I fetched a chisel and a hammer. I asked my son to hold the bottle still while I tapped under the cork.

'What are you talking about? To blame for what?'

I said that in the old days turning on the radio after the working day was a treat. You had time to listen for three-quarters of an hour, before bed. But now six-year-olds are connected to everything all the time; soon they will even be linked to the future. You'll be able to tell from a foetus whether it will become a great fiddler or whether its strengths are more in bouncing a basketball or maybe in empathetic listening. If no gifts are discernible, the parents will be forced to wonder whether their child has any future in this world.

Young people have plenty of free time, from waking to sleeping. But do they know what to do when the electricity ends? Does the government have an archive copy of everything that is hidden on computers? Do the archives contain beam-carvers' horsemen, pump-station specialists or people who'll use moss for insulation when industry finally runs out of fuel or the Chinese say they can't be bothered to provide us with clothes and machines any more? Do it yourselves. Now we're going to feed and clothe our own citizens, who have been making things for you for a few generations.

Our wheat has been sold abroad, the idea being that we can always import frozen pizza and icy fish cubes. Oil has been used in the hope that the solar car will soon conquer the world. There are no cattle, except in huge pastures somewhere in Uruguay or Argentina, because raising them there is apparently cheaper. This is the kind of world that is wanted by people for whom we intended something quite different. That's why

generations are always stupid. They never really pull in
the same direction as the last; instead, hopes and wishes
are great and oars are pulled in different directions.
The boat goes in a circle. A card-index sure is an easy
way of keeping records. For me, the blank sides of the
advertisements you get in the post are enough – you can
design a warehouse shelf or a house on one of those.
Your own memory is the best record.

When everything is kept on computers, people don't
delve in their memories any more and they become
stupid. When computers fail, people fail too, because
they have no back-up. They don't know where they are
without a map program, and they don't have feelings
without TV series. That's what human life is like now,
in the year two thousand and however many it may be,
a lot.

'I agree that the information society is still, like, in
development,' my son said. 'But maybe it isn't . . . quite
so straightforward.'

They goggle at their little devices and don't look the
person they're speaking to in the eye any more. If you
agree something, all you need is a meeting of the eyes
and a proper handshake, but that's forgotten because
a swipe and a stroke are enough. You sure do lose
your faith in the other party if you shake their hand
and it's limp and sweaty, like a dead fish. This was
the problem, for example, with the candidate in the
municipal elections, from Perälä, whom I considered a
trustworthy woman until I found myself on her election

stand. I took the coffee I was offered and declined a badge. As I left we shook hands. Her hand was so limp that I didn't bother to vote in the next three elections.

'I wonder if I've heard what you're talking about before,' my son says. 'It seems to me I've read a lot of books on this subject written by you and always with the same arguments. Everything used to be better than it is now.'

Finally the cork of the ink bottle began to come loose. My son held it and I twisted it with my better hand.

No one needs to write a book about what I have to say; instead, a guide called *How to Be an Ordinary Person – Ordinary is Enough* should be distributed to every home. Why not put it on the computers too. How to live wisely and not stupidly, a kind of guide to living. My son was silent for quite a long time, as if he was waiting to see if I would say anything else.

I stuck the nib of the pen into the ink. It was completely solid.

I would need to go into town to get some better ink.

I don't dance, I don't sing, I don't party

As we drove along, I explained to my son how to change up from second gear to third and that it's worth using the engine to brake. You'd have to be a sheik swimming in money to wear out your brake pads on purpose. And it's ecological and economical, after all, to anticipate and use the clutch.

Although on the other hand it could be best to use up all the fossil fuels as soon as possible. There are so many engineers and mathematicians working out that birch sap or mud soup can be used to make a fantastic combined fuel. Someone invented petrol, after all; windmills have been known about since the beginning of time.

'Dad, errm . . . You seem to have such an awful lot to say these days. Could you be . . . quiet . . . for a moment. Don't be offended, will you? But you went for decades with only, like, twenty-nine words.'

I understood what my son meant. It couldn't be more annoying if I sounded like my mother-in-law. I decided to take a little nap, because I've always been able to get to sleep on the Kuuspohja stretch, ever since I was a little boy. In the late Fifties there was so much to do that I learned to take a nap as I walked from the building site or home from the fields.

Now I dozed off again, I don't know for how long. I didn't dream, because I don't dream. When I woke with a start, I noticed that the car wasn't moving. We hadn't reached our destination; we were at the point where Storm Tapani had felled the forest like hay.

I asked my son how long I'd been asleep.

He wasn't beside me; instead, he was standing outside the car, by the side of the forest. I rolled the window down and asked him to start driving again. We didn't have all day. I had my will to write, the potatoes to cook and the news to watch. My son turned to look at me and put his phone back in his pocket.

He had tears in his eyes.

He got back into the driver's seat. He didn't say anything, just continued the journey. He still didn't understand that he should slip the gears.

What should I have asked him? What do you ask your own son when he's been crying? I asked why he made such a bad change from second to third, not realising how important it was that he should let the clutch out properly. We'd talked about it right after driving school.

Cars are like people, you can always understand them if you steer them and listen to them for long enough. Everyone has their sweet spot, and you have to know how to tickle it, fluff it up or stroke it with a feather. For me, it's the lower back. The children walked on it when they were small and until they got bigger – and the smallest person in our family was my wife.

It's strange how many places are affected by the kind of back pain you get when coppicing. It can go to your head and to your toes. You sleep badly and become irritable and at work you saw crookedly and the foreman thinks you have a hangover and your wife thinks you're mad and you just bite your lip and wonder why you can't just pull your spine out like a sore tooth.

It's a strange sight when there's a tear on a man's cheek.

You should surreptitiously wipe it away on your sleeve and say something got in your eye or that it's the frost. You shouldn't let the whole world see it, or me. Young people have read too much, watched too much television; they believe in women's tales and not men's actions. Since they were children they've been told that they can speak, that they must cry and that hugging is compulsory.

Not that anyone forbade it before.

It's just that there wasn't time.

The men of today don't know how to live normally any more, because they have to be half women. They have to cook food, change nappies and clean floors. They're important jobs, like handing out water bottles at a marathon, but why's it necessary, afterwards, to gossip and cry? It's no longer enough to be happy or sad; instead, you have to know exactly *why* you're happy or sad. An ordinary person's sorrows are paraded in front of everyone even though there's only one thing you do when you're happy. You drink coffee with cream.

And what you do when you're sad: you drink black coffee.

Things happen.

I remember how much my daughter-in-law wanted to fuss over me when my wife was taken to the care home. She was worried that I wouldn't be able to survive from day to day in my grief and loneliness. And it didn't feel good, of course not, but when did life feel good? Life doesn't ask us what we want, it doesn't let us choose. There are twists and turns. War comes, Olympic victories. A child. Colour television. A child dies. Another child comes. A burst water-pipe. A grandchild. Old age. The Finnish Union Bank is replaced by the wondrous Merita Bank and the SMP, the Finnish Rural Party, by the Reform Group. Illness. Death, too, comes, to plants, political parties, Olympic victors. And me. Life doesn't improve by standing still, nor does grief soften by wallowing in it. I certainly wouldn't say the world is perfect, because there are bad things about it too, but there's a lot about it that is OK too.

My son looked at me for a long time. I suppose I had said some of this out loud.

'Where did we get to?' my son asked.

I said the gutters needed to be cleared. Otherwise they would break. Love can certainly last, if gutters can.

'I suppose they'll last, I suppose they make them out of something like plastic . . .'

I asked if they were getting a divorce. That's what you do, these days, after all, after a certain number of years. Was that what he was crying about? In the old days you bought your wife a brooch or went on holiday to the seaside where the water was warm; now, you get a divorce and joint custody.

'I don't quite . . . understand.'

Even I have cried as an adult. Although I sure don't remember why. The year was 'Sixty-two. I didn't want to think about it, so I broke my own promise and spoke again. I said that at this time of year it's worth taking the shortcut via Mölhönperä.

'What's it got to do with the time of year?'

Because there may be swans in the field. If there are, you should mark it on your calendar.

'You've said yourself that it's the driver who chooses the route and the radio station,' my son said.

Of course he does when I'm at the wheel. What will the world come to if sons and wives get to choose the route? Suddenly we will be stopping at gift shops, fun fairs, we will be having accidents and causing expense for tax-payers, of whom I am one. My son sighed and shook his head. That means the same as grunting does for me. It means that although we speak the same language we are to each other like the inhabitants of Ovamboland and Greenland. Sometimes the journey of one person to another is many miles even though that one person has come from the other.

Let it be said that I'm not good at comforting. It's easier for me to listen to commentaries and the shipping forecast than to grief. We know what loss, pain and suffering are like; I have seen them all, up close and for long periods, during my life, but I don't like to spend time with them in the company of anyone but myself. You have the strength to bear your own grief, to put it in a wheelbarrow and take it to the compost heap. There's far too much weight to bear in another person's grief.

My wife knows how to let me be. She kept her distance, a few metres or a couple of rooms. Brought me coffee and cake. Started talking to me only when my cough began to sound right again or when I asked the quiz questions from the newspaper. I knew the answers about politics and sport, my wife knew geography and these pop and film stars.

I know now, at this age and too late, that I didn't know how to go to my wife when she needed me. That was why my wife watched the programmes where men were able to talk and took their wives out to dinner in places where candle flames flickered. I wondered what that cost the licence-fee payer, and said so out loud. I didn't realise that my wife might have needed something more from me than a house extension. Or the time when my only friend Yrjänä's dog died and I helped mend his roof and Yrjänä tried to talk to me about his dog, but I slipped off quickly to fetch the nails or realised that it was time for the radio news, and after that the television news, and after that the radio. In the sauna Yrjänä drank twice as much booze than ever before and muttered that it should have been him that went and not his dog. I remarked on how well the chimney drew even though it was already ninety years old and it was nearly time for the news.

We do not grieve for the loss of dogs or of people, but for ourselves. We who are left here and all the things that remind us of those who got away. I sure wasn't in the mood for this kind of thing. I thought about my will, which would be good and surprising like Veikko Huovinen's three best books.

I asked my son to drive via Koulutie road, because there are always roadworks on Kauppakatu Street. I sure don't understand how it helps anyone to make a hole in the road, put council workers at the bottom for a year to have a look and then fill it in again. I told him to take the next left.

'Why?'

The office supplies shop is there.

'It isn't.'

It was.

'Not any more.'

Where the sign once said 'R. Ritola Dealership and Supplies' was now an AA office. I tried to remember what those As meant, but all that came to mind was the skier Asko Autio, champion of the fifty kilometre cross-country ski race.

'The office supplies shop was last here around the 1990s,' my son said. 'When the whole structure of Finland's workforce changed.'

I asked where were we going to find ink then? My son switched off the engine and asked if we couldn't just forget about the whole damned will. I asked him to shut up and thought. It was music therapy day on my wife's ward and I don't go then. I might be forced to dance, and I don't dance. Or sing. Or clap my hands together to order. I don't scream for joy without a reason.

I asked my son to search his touch phone for the nearest office supplies store. Two hundred kilometres, it said. I would get back in time for tomorrow's lunchtime feed, and my son would be home before evening.

My favourite subject was handicrafts

My son handed me the phone because there was no holder for it in my car. Why should a car have a phone-holder? The towing hook, the glove compartment and the tailgate, those I understand, but even ski carriers are incomprehensible to me. Skis belong on your feet. You ski on virgin snow or on a ski run close to home; you don't carry them on your car roof to northern ski centres or groomed ski slopes. If you really have a yearning for Lapland, then go ahead and ski there.

'Just hold on to it,' my son said.

The phone spoke good Finnish in a woman's voice: 'In three hundred metres turn left at the roundabout. Then, drive one hundred and six kilometres.' I asked how the phone could know where we were going. What if we changed our minds on the way, as young people always do? Did the phone know the cost of the roundabout, because in my opinion traffic lights would have been a much better choice.

'There's a satellite.'

In the phone?

'In the sky.'

Why?

'So that the phone can . . . so that the navigator can work.'

Navi what?

'Gator. The maps program. Look, I don't know. Can you just hold on to it.'

I rolled the window down and looked at the sky. You can't see the stars any more; the lights of villages, towns and petrol stations hide their glimmer. Today's Marco Polos and Vikings would have to follow service station signs instead of stars, and would then claim they were the first to find the Hollola ABC. Even if it was actually Heinola. They would go crazy the same way as America and the Indians. The Vikings wouldn't even be interested in where they had got to as long as they could take the male clients of the ABC as slaves, the women as wives and the children as their own.

'It sure is hard for me to see the Vikings and the ABC in the same picture,' my son blustered.

But today, from up there among the constellations, it's a device that tells us who we are and where we're going. I suppose it's useful. With such a device you could find the quickest way out of a hypermarket. If you set off along the wrong aisle from the dairy section toward the till, you end up where you started as the loudspeaker announces, ladies and gentlemen, our store will be closing in five minutes. I asked whether the device had any opinions on the matter, or better suggestions. Could it tell us the quickest way to get ink for my Pelikan?

The streetlights ended and the car was now lit only by the phone's screen. We were driving along the grey road, in the midst of the green forest – in the phone's opinion the only car on the road, marked by an arrow on the screen. I assumed my son knew the road without directions and put the phone in the glove compartment.

Then I took a headlamp from my pocket and fitted it to my head. I turned to my son and asked him if the light was on.

'Aargh! Help! Turn it off!'

A person should always carry in their pocket a screwdriver, two hundred Finnish marks and a headlamp. In euros that's thirty-three point-thirty-three, assuming the exchange rate is one to six. Your nerves must be strong but at the bottom of the cliff there needs to be a foam rubber mattress so you don't hurt your back if you fall. An open mind. That's the way to get through most things. Post-war reconstruction, the Finno-Soviet Treaty, and today's nonsense.

The oncoming cars flashed their headlights. My son said the reason was my headlamp, which would be dazzling not only him but also any oncoming lorries. I found a dial on the side of the lamp with which I could lower the wattage a little and directed the light beam into my lap. I rummaged in my pocket for three pieces of squared paper.

'Dad, could you please just calmly switch that light off? Don't turn your head, just switch it off using that button.'

What button does he mean?

'Any old shi— fu— button.'

But I can't see to read if there's no light.

'Honestly, listen, this could be serious.'

I turned my head towards my son and said that I had to go through the draft of my obituary. He began to shout and I worried that he might be about to cry. A shouting, weeping man was in collision with an articulated lorry, his father wearing a maximum-power lamp on his forehead. That is what they'd write.

I pressed one of the buttons. It didn't put the lamp out; instead, blue and then red lights began to flash inside the car. Then the lamp went out, but the flashing continued in my eyes, and I am sure my son's, because the car began to shimmy along the central line. My son suggested using his phone; it would give enough light to read a piece of paper.

Following my son's instructions, I touched the phone's torch on button. We wouldn't have lit anything with my old grey Ericsson dial phone or found our way anywhere. Or else we would have had to tape my Airam torch to the phone and use the world's longest extension lead.

'What papers have you got now? Could you please keep them on your own side?'

That's exactly where they are. It's completely wrong that the dead person is always written about in the third person.

'Who?'

In obituaries. Everyone. Kekkonen. Khomeini. Arvi Lind, when his time comes. Me. He this and he that and that Jarmo Olavi Höpäjäinen was a wrestler in his youth, a fertiliser expert as an adult and in retirement a nature enthusiast. But was he really? Who will know when there is no Jarmo Olavi Höpäjäinen to tell us, since he never revealed his true self to anyone? Wisdom after the event is stupidity after the event, certainly in obituaries.

It sure is best for a person to tell their own story. I trust my own words more than a poet's verses, a relative's embellishments or a reporter's statistics. That is why, for a number of years, I have been preparing my own text. I have underlined wrongly written obituaries in the newspapers in the library and copied the few good ones. The best was Hilpi Maaretti Ryönä's obituary; I just can't remember why, or where I put it.

The draft is written in pencil and if only we could get some ink for my pen, I would write out a fair copy and lodge it in the bank's safety deposit box. I will take a copy round to the local newspaper's offices with an instruction to say it can be opened only when I am no longer alive. My son can say whether the capital letters, commas and proper names are written correctly, as there's no trusting newspapers' proofreaders any more. Because there aren't any.

There are always employee co-operation negotiations and as a result the following day a thinner and poorer newspaper in which the wrong things are written about wrongly. Last year they spelt cocoa with a 'k'. The week before they wrote memorandums instead of memoranda. I really don't believe in portents of the end of the world, but that's what it felt like. Eventually all that will be left in the newspaper business will be the consultants who suggested all the redundancies. They will begin to make each other redundant and, wearing tattered designer suits, briefcase in hand, will stalk the perimeters of the glass buildings competing with the rats and local riffraff for something to eat.

'I've also been following the newspaper redundancies with some concern.'

I died when I had lived for long enough. I sure had my boots on. Good boots, bought at Pielavesi in 'Sixty-two.

I was born on the fourth of June at the beginning of the Thirties in the same place as I died. At home. Or, more accurately, in the sauna. If you take care of a sauna stove it will last for a human life. The family was

also from there, because everyone comes from home.
Except those who were born on a journey. But even
then we are usually going home or wondering where
we will build the place we will call home.

I asked my son how it sounded so far. Did the ideas
meander as strangely and lengthily as the Porvoonjoki
river? My son said he thought it was a gripping piece
of writing. I don't know whether he was serious or
indulging in his generation's birth defect, irony. I'd
checked what it meant in the dictionary. It means that
you're not responsible for your own words, but say one
thing and mean another. When I was young irony hadn't
even been invented. You said what you meant, or else
kept quiet. More difficult things were pondered in silence
or else left to brew for the rest of your life. That sort of
thing sure leads to a build-up of mould, but that's part of
life, even if it shouldn't be part of a building. I told my
son that in the next paragraph I wanted to deal quickly
with my family.

They weren't all nice people, but generally they
looked after each other rather than abandoning them.
I inherited a fur hat and once I even got some pancake.
I didn't like my uncle Simeoni or the uncle who had
something wrong with one of his legs. Their heads were
messed up in the war. Or were they just unpleasant
people to begin with. Of the following I have nothing
either good or bad to say: Luoma, Antti Pennanen,

Vinski Tuukkainen and the cousin they called a baboon.
Mother had warm hands and father taught me to light
firewood from the top, not the bottom.

My son tried to remember the name of my mother, his
grandmother, and when granny died and whether he had
ever caught sight of the unpleasant relatives I mentioned.
I told him how he had burst into tears as soon as he saw
Uncle Urpo in the summer of 'Seventy-something. He
ran to the back seat of the Escort, locked the doors and
refused to come back to the party. I'm also fond of getting
into that car; I do not like the very loud people who are
always to be found at parties. They fill the shared silence
with cackles and talk about how wonderful their children
are. Our Jarkko played the violin at the spring festival,
they say, but forget to mention that it was painful to the
ears and that he did it against his will. Another thing
I do not like is the bottle of booze hidden in the stack of
firewood, and this being the case I have to sit among the
babbling women and look as if I'm listening to their talk
even though I'm really trying to count all the berries on
the blackcurrant bush.

I do remember one good party in my life, apart from
my wedding. A boy from our village came eighth in the
Olympics ski biathlon and for that reason the entire
village was served coffee and cake in the town hall.
The skier sat in a leather armchair and was given a
combined stereo-radio. With my wife beside me and my
son in my arms I shook hands with the man and asked

how he managed to get that fourth shot, that Rauno. Or was it Teijo. Or perhaps Kaaleppi. I also asked which furniture shop the armchair was from, Isku or Asko.

'I don't remember anything like that,' my son said. 'Maybe it was Pekka who was there. But go on, this is beginning to get interesting.'

Then came the missing years, in other words the war. I helped mother a lot, as my big brothers were at the front. Once, when I was coming from the berry forest, I found some chocolate beside a spruce tree, with a label that said something in Russian. No one believed me, as I ate the chocolate immediately and used the wrapper as kindling because I had to light the campfire. Must have been a Russian spy.

'I've always been kind of interested in micro and macro history,' my son interjected. 'I took History as a secondary subject. There should be more studies of just this kind of home-front folklore.'

If you've lived through something it isn't history or folklore, but life. My son went a bit quiet. I was afraid he might start to cry and returned to my text.

At primary school I was the only pupil who was better than my friend Yrjänä. I would have gone to secondary school, but my father thought it wasn't for the likes of us. Mother would have let me go.

'Did it feel bad that someone else was allowed to go but you weren't?' asked my son. 'I mean . . . did you feel any bitterness. Overtly or . . .'

I didn't understand the question. Drinks can be bitter, or Juha Mieto's missing the gold in the fifteen-kilometre ski race at the Lake Placid Winter Olympics by a hundredth of a second in 1980. That sure would have been bitter if he hadn't borne it so well.

I skied eight thousand seven hundred and sixty-five kilometres in four years. My favourite subject was handicrafts.

'You mean woodwork,' my son asked.

I shook my head, because of course I meant sewing.

'Sewing? Or what's its proper name. Textiles. Did you really do textiles in the Thirties?'

The workshop was only just being built beside the out-building and there was no space for woodwork apart from the endless forests around us, from where we had to fetch firewood, berries for eating and leaves for pressing. According to Mr Toikkanen everyone should be able to knit themselves a woolly hat, because you never knew if you would end up a widower or be a bachelor all your life, as he was. Knitting was different from woodwork or hammering hot metal or chopping a log, which were familiar and necessary at home. I would be able to do them all throughout my life, whereas I might knit just this once. And it was nice to make a garment out of thread in the warm classroom.

I can reveal things like this because they will be read only when I am no longer here. It's my son who will have to bear the shame.

'No, quite the opposite. That's like . . . wild, I mean liberating.'

Does he mean the fact that he will have to bear the shame?

'No, the fact that you like knitting. I'll have to tell the children . . .'

I pointed out that I liked it just that one time. There's no need to make a song and dance about it or give it special significance. Today's children don't understand that people have always been the same. They've liked all sorts of things, genders, spice mixes and makes of car, even if they pretend otherwise. The liberalism my son goes on about has always been present in some people, just like the more poisonous way of thinking in which your own garden, wife, child and parish are best and other people's gardens, for instance, are eyesores.

In the main, the world is made up of sensible people like me. There are people like me in Iran, North Korea, Russia, Lahti, Oulainen, Upper Volta and the Congo. They're just not the first to go on television shouting and shooting their assault rifles in the air when they hurt their ankles or their home is hit by an ally or rebel missile. Sensible people sit in the background drinking coffee or some strange-tasting tea and wonder what all the noise is about. What's worth shouting in the squares and newspapers is a different matter. If, in 1942, I had said out loud how pleasant it was to knit a woolly hat, it's unlikely that in later life I would have been a valued joiner at Koistinen Builders. In my youth there was no college a boy child could go to to further his studies in woolly hat making.

'It's still quite funny. You knitting . . .'

I urged my son to take into account the fact that I was not this age then. It was not my life's dream in the way that, for example, riding a pig was, but that is a completely different story. I made one solitary woolly hat, and if I had made another it would have become boring. I was a child. There's nothing funny about it. I told my son to forget the whole thing or I would cross it out of my obituary. He nodded, although I could see from his eyes that he wanted to laugh.

I've always had jobs to do. I got my first pay packet when I was nine years old. I didn't always feel like getting up in the morning, but it was better than staying at home where it was cold. We didn't have electronic devices or a Soda-Stream or duvets in those days. These are the jobs I've done:

- *abbatoir assistant*
- *sawmill worker*
- *surveyor*
- *trustee*

- *butcher*
- *photographer*
- *smallholder*
- *government worker*
- *civil activist*
- *chauffeur's assistant*

My son was astonished. He was interested in what part civil activism had played in my life and where I'd even managed to hear the term. Well, there's stuff about it on the television, in the newspaper and on the radio all the time and I've sure written letters to the editor. Plenty of times, over the petrol pump, I've grumbled about the state of the world, Kolehmainen's stupidity and helpfully offered my suggestions as to how to put things right. I really believe that I've achieved more good things than the guys in woolly jumpers who scale oil platforms or chain themselves to trees.

'So are you talking about those Arctic areas . . .'

I sure wasn't, but now you mention it. When you're up against a country where wrong opinions are rewarded with a bullet in the neck, I for one wouldn't like to see my children's children protesting against anything. It's a country where yesterday's wrong opinion can be tomorrow's right one. And anyway, worrying may be pointless in the sense that drilling for oil will end when the oil ends. After that all the alternative technology will be taken into use.

Wind power, wave power and solar power. Oil was a turbo-accelerator that helped the human race get a head-start over everyone else and each other. Now we should learn how to brake so we don't all fly through the windscreen.

'In a way you're completely wrong,' said my son. 'And in a way, right. There are so many factors to take into account in the climate debate . . . But what do you mean, a photographer? You know you never agree either to take pictures or to be in them.'

It's a long story, involving a bottle of potato wine, a taxi trip to Kerava and a certain medium-sized track-and-field event at the Zoo playing field in Helsinki.

'But surely you never visited the metropolitan area until we moved there?'

Well, we sure didn't call Helsinki the metropolitan area in the Fifties. And I had to go somewhere to find my wife. Or was it that she found me?

My son turned to look at me, but I told him to keep his eyes on the road.

'Did you meet in Helsinki? Was Mum from Helsinki? Why am I never told anything?'

Did you ever ask?

My son was silent.

I won that camera in the only card game of my life, from Manu Hurrila on the steps of the grocer's shop. In those days you sure did have to think hard about what was worth taking a picture of, because film was the price of gold. That's how it should still be today – people should have the right to eight photographs over their whole life.

I went on with my obituary.

In writing lessons I could do perfect loops on the letter 's'. Both big and small. Why is it that these days people only print? The loops on the letters are beautiful frivolities, of which there should be three in life. Telemark skiing, lace and the loops on letters.

Before and after school we worked. From spring to late autumn there were jobs in the house, then paid work. The forest was our bank, there was plenty there to fell, saw and float down the river. You could hide there, and get lost. If you followed the river far enough, you got to the factory. There would have been work there too. But I preferred to start my family on my own lands. My homeland.

I found a wife. We sat in the grandstand and laughed. Drank a lot of coffee.

She baked the best cardamom pulla *buns in the world.*

At this point I had to stop for a moment and look at the road, which was located in the present, unlike what I was writing, which was located in other parts of my life.

We had children. One did the long-jump, seven metres thirty, and now lives in Belgium. Highly educated, as all sorts of schooling became possible for everyone. It's a good thing, of course, but they don't come home very often any more. They have so many courses to go to, so many off-site meetings, so many performance appraisals. They have under-floor heating, all my children. We had rugs on the floor. And on the wall.

'Was that it?' my son asked. 'That can't be all? Dad? I'd like some more detail. Like at the beginning, and more information about the relatives. The beginning and the end are a bit out of balance . . . kinda structurally . . .'

P.S. Don't come to the grave every week. There are more living people in life who it's worth remembering.

We were quiet together, I felt in a good way.

'Yes, it sure is . . . can you say beautiful?'

That was my life and that was what my life was like. My son can write about his own life according to his own sense of the world. You can't write this kind of thing with a spirit level. My son said it might interest the reader to know where my wife and I met and what it was that made me fall in love with her. What it felt like when the children were born.

'What, errm, did it feel like when I was born?' my son said quietly.

Freezing.

'What?!'

We were building the Sohjojoki river bridge when they called the building site office to say it was a boy. Thirty-two degrees of frost and the concrete frozen. All you have to do is stop digging and you feel cold in conditions like that.

'You just can't express your feelings, can you?' my son asked. 'I certainly remember exactly what I felt when each of my children was born.'

I remember my grandchildren, too, there's been more time to wait and listen. But when you had to work there wasn't much time for analysing emotions. If it was cold it was cold, until it was warm. If it never got warm then your fingers and toes dropped off with frostbite. That was what happened to Vihtori Kauto that time.

Suddenly there was a strange voice in the car, and a vibration in my lap. It was the device. It had something to say. In five hundred metres take the right-hand lane and turn right. I folded my obituary contentedly back into my pocket and tried to keep my mind on the right track. The editors and people at the local paper would be able to read it and think: that was what he was like, and he could have revealed a bit more. But it's best not to reveal everything; that leaves an itch.

My son took a few wrong turnings down one-way streets so that when we reached the household appliance shop it was already closed.

He squeezed the steering wheel and stared ahead without a word. The phone rang, and I passed it over.

'Well, I don't know!' was the only thing he said. And then: 'I don't think we'll ever get out of here.'

He thrust the phone back into my lap and started the car. My son tried to calm himself down and asked me whether we should drive back.

I had to do what you have to remember to do with children, even if the child is forty-five-years-old. Get their blood sugar back in order, because otherwise you're going to have to deal with crying, kicking and refusing to get dressed.

Is the Escort here?

We sure aren't hotel people. My wife and I spent our honeymoon in a fine four-storey building, but it was difficult being served by strangers. We tried to rest in the soft beds, but you get tired of that kind of thing, especially when you are constantly worrying the whole time about whether your cousin's son can milk the cows or whether Tuulikki is going to give birth on our wedding night. My wife fretted about whether the berry harvest was going to spoil over those two nights. At half-past four in the morning we set off back home and it definitely was easier when we had to do everything ourselves again.

My son wanted a separate room. I asked if I looked like a millionaire, did I look like Vesa Keskinen, who exploits human stupidity and sells useless screwdrivers in three currencies? I certainly had no intention of throwing my money around, even if the children would ultimately inherit it.

'So, one room for two people?' asked the child-like, smiling girl behind the counter. 'Separate beds, I'm sure? Have you visited us before?'

We had been here in the sense that we knew the hotel's sign, which illuminated the bypass and blocked out the old church behind it. But I had a special offer coupon and was hoping that it would get us a good reduction.

The receptionist took the coupon and looked at it for a remarkably long time. She glanced at me and she glanced at the coupon. I asked her to ring the price up on the till so that we could get some rest.

The receptionist went into the next room to show the coupon to her manager. There was a little outburst of laughter. The girl gave the piece of paper back to me apologetically, saying that the coupon appeared to be from the year 'Eighty-six or 'Eighty-seven. Of course it was, I'd cut it out of *Apu* magazine, along the dotted lines, to wait for the right day. Now was the right day. There was no mention of when the offer closed, and it clearly said one night for two hundred Finnish marks and two litres of lemonade as a special gift. I sure don't drink fizzy drinks, but my son could take them home to his children.

'So, we do have an offer of fifteen per cent if you have a membership card. Do you have a membership card?'

Membership cards are an instrument for fleecing honest people and spying on shopping habits.

'But you can sign up for a membership card here. It doesn't cost anything, and you can take advantage of the offer. You'll receive an advantage card like this one. You can use it for the beer and refreshments in the mini-bar.'

You really don't need special offers in a place you only visit once. With their memberships and their plastic cards they're trying to get you to take one bottle from the mini-bar and then eight and then finally you want to pour all the tiny booze bottles down your throat – the ones that look like toys in a big man's hand. You stagger from the lift to the lobby as if the whole world belonged to you. You ask the way to the bar and whether the girl will come with you. You take some unknown Sirpa back to your room, wake up beside her in the morning and everything is black. In the car park a sports car bought on hire purchase awaits you. Shame seeps through your temples.

'My father means he doesn't particularly want to join.'

And with the membership card the hotel owner is able to find out what kind of person I am. Whether I shower for more than six minutes and whether I like soft pillows or hard ones and whether I snore.

'This is just an S-card,' said the receptionist.

I asked what my Escort had to do with it. I wondered whether we were being watched by that satellite up there and whether tomorrow I would begin to receive targeted mail in my inbox. I looked at my son and enquired whether he knew anything about this.

'S-card,' my son explained. 'Not Escort.'

I sure didn't understand a thing.

'Well, OK, yes,' said the assistant. 'You can think about it. You can get the advantages when you check out too . . .'

The receptionist handed us the forms. You had to tick whether the purpose of the journey was work or leisure. I wasn't sure, so I wrote buying a bottle of ink and writing a will in small but clear handwriting. The receptionist gave us a card, which was apparently a key, and told us that breakfast was served from six to ten o'clock. The sauna was open until nine in the evening and from seven in the morning. I asked if there was a swimming pool in the hotel.

'Well, yes there is!' said the receptionist, overjoyed.

It sure is senseless to build indoor pools and keep the water warm. The result is water damage and the kind of bills run up by sheikhs who build ski centres in the middle of the desert. Are the people who deserve to be there in the pool – children learning to stay on the surface, car accident victims learning to walk again or people who have lost their limbs in war, lightly floating? Certainly not. In the pool float commercial travellers, cognac in their heads, in their stomachs steaks flambéed with more of the cognac.

'So yes, absolutely,' said the hotel worker, and my son pulled me toward the lift.

My son pushed the key-card into the slot and pressed the button. He didn't say anything, and I didn't care to say anything either. Lifts don't jerk into motion or bump as they arrive at their destination any more. There's no gate that you open or where a child's football, or Kiikko Hulttinen's hand, can get caught, the hand that after that could no longer make a catch in baseball.

Our room was on the fifth floor and from its windows you could see other buildings with five floors.

My son slumped on to the bed while I made an inspection. I began with the bathroom. Soft, large towels. Yrjänä always pinched towels on his Leningrad trips, and when I used to go to his house to use the sauna in the summer, those towels reminded us of all kinds of incidents. For example when the military police took Erkki Pöyhönen away after he tried to buy himself a wife and a Lada with six packets of tights.

After the lavatory I inspected the desk. A couple of blank pieces of paper and three ball-point pens with the name of the hotel written on them. It's not worth putting these in your pocket, because then at home they will see that you've been lounging around in a hotel and stealing their pens. Next to the blotter was a kettle with instant coffee bags, tea bags, packets of sugar and powdered cream. I wasn't envious of the bloated commercial traveller who had to drink ersatz coffee every morning.

Eventually I found a folder with emergency exit instructions, a map of the town and the restaurant menu. I gave it to my son and asked him to work out which dish had the best combination of price, quality and carbohydrates.

While my son read the menu I went through the cupboards. There was a safe, as if I had valuable items apart from my obituary with me – it was securely locked in the Escort's glove compartment. In the next cupboard was an extra duvet and a pillow, beside them a Bible. I asked whether my son remembered Zebedee's sons.

'There's a chicken basket here. Would you eat it? A twenty per cent reduction using the S-card; a pity we don't have one.'

Zebulon, Dan, Naphtali and the rest, why do I know them all? There's one good piece of advice in that big book, which a person can use to get by in every country, job, trip, nursery, factory, football pitch and bank counter. Do unto others as you would have them do unto you.

'I might fancy the pizza if it's vegetarian . . .'

But the problem is, of course, that few people wish for themselves what I wish for myself. A hard pillow, not a soft one. I want to die on my own terms and in my own time, not in a hospital bed. I wonder if this even occurred to Jesus the Nazarene when he pronounced the sentences that lasted from one millennium to the next. I don't think so.

I set the Bible down and wondered what other books a hotel room should have, if having a book were compulsory. A maintenance manual for the Ford Escort is always necessary. Veikko Huovinen's *Fatty Liver* and the other story where they do some pickling, that would be good to have translated into every language – for example the Sámi language, which I follow on the local news bulletins. There are stories on a personal scale, like the one about how in Sodankylä the youths drew rude pictures on snowmobiles or that in Finnmark a wolf ate eight reindeer and now the Sámis's livelihood is threatened. When a hurricane or a dictator wipes out an entire nation and civilisation, you sure can't begin to comprehend such things.

In the last cupboard is a dressing gown, fluffy as a kitten. I've certainly never worn a dressing gown. My son suggested that the sausage basket could be a good alternative for me; he himself would be fine with the clear salmon broth.

I went back into the bathroom and changed out of my own clothes and into the dressing gown; I put a pair of slippers on my feet. I looked in the mirror, slightly ashamed and much amused. I asked if my son wanted to come with me. There were two dressing gowns and next to the shower there were bags to protect long hair if you didn't want to get it wet.

'Where are we supposed to be going? Aren't we going to have something to eat?'

Change of plan. Let's go swimming first.

'Swimming?'

Didn't you hear what the girl at reception said? It's included in the price. If you don't use what's provided for you, it's wasteful. We're not wastrels.

'I, errm, I'm going to, I mean, have a rest for a moment. Errm, is that OK? Can you find your way to the spa? Are you sure you want to go right now?'

I've sure found my way to more difficult places than a hotel sauna. Once I pulled a horse out of a bog and afterwards the horse had to pull me out.

Life is short, bar bills long

Such is the extent to which the world has lost its mind that it doesn't understand what happens if the bottom of a swimming pool on the top floor gives way. Chlorinated water will flow down like a Niagara, destroying everything in its path. Fitted carpets, safe deposit boxes, the New Testaments of the Gideon brothers and holidaymakers' best clothes. The insurance company will pay the claims, but then raise my premium.

To judge by the clothes left outside, there was one bather in the sauna apart from me. I chose a place on one side of the dressing room and now I understood why the bathing spaces were located on the top floors.

Beyond the windows, in the dark, the town could be seen, illuminated by the evening lights. It was magnificent, if completely pointless. But people like light better than darkness. They like good things better than bad things. If you ask my wife, she likes chocolate better than gherkins.

It all began with the campfire. Before that there was the sun, but it was feared because even *Homo erectus* cannot influence a ball of fire and at night it disappears completely, and there in the darkness the dads, mums and brats of the Stone Age had to get some sleep. There was reason to be afraid of it, too, as its temperature is around fifteen million degrees. You sure couldn't work in the fields in that kind of heat, however many siestas you took, however many supplements or days off.

The blaze of the town reminds a person of the blaze of a campfire. You know that warmth is nearby, and other members of your species. You know that you're not about to die from a sabre-tooth tiger attack or from hunger, as long as you can get to the next campfire. A juicy muskrat is roasting on the neighbour's embers, and you may be able to get a piece of flank if you have a sharp stone or a flower to give in return. Of course they may also be hostile folk, who will greet you with a blow to the temples with a wooden club.

Do lighting designers know anything about this? Do they think about it? They sure don't know how silly their profession sounds to my ears.

I took off my dressing gown.

Then the phone rang and there was a vibration in my trousers. Why did I have a vibrating phone in my trouser pocket? I keep my phone on the dresser at home. Because it was my son's phone and it had stayed in my pocket after the car journey.

It took me a moment to answer, as I had to slide my finger across the glass surface of the screen.

'Where the hell are you?'

At the swimming pool. Who's speaking?

'At the swimming pool? What do you mean, who's speaking?'

I'm speaking.

'Where?'

To be clear, we're at the hotel swimming pool. Too high up, I don't know how many storeys. A swimming pool sure does belong in the cellar.

'You were supposed to be with your dad.'

What do you mean?

'We agreed that you would go ahead and I would follow on afterwards. Are you thinking straight?'

My dad has been pushing up the daisies for a long time.

'Wasn't he perfectly healthy . . . Is that why you're not here?'

Forty years he's been dead. Is that how long it's been? A long time, anyway. He was a perfectly healthy man for seventy-one, even if he sometimes smoked, but they all did in those days. In his seventy-second year he got a stomach ache, and that's what took him away. They found cancer in the post-mortem. He never said anything about it, just sometimes complained about stomach acid.

'Who am I talking to here?'

Who am I talking to?

'Liisa.'

Oh. Right. My daughter-in-law?

'It's you?!'

It's me, good evening, we haven't seen each other for ages.

'Where's Hessu?'

He stayed in the room.

'What bloody room?'

A woman sure shouldn't curse like that.

'Tell me which town you're in. I need to talk to him straight away.'

We're in the big smoke. In an extraordinary hotel where they won't take coupons, but an Escort is apparently acceptable. You wouldn't believe how pushy they are.

'Wait there. Don't go anywhere!'

Where would we go, since our room is paid for? It doesn't open again until tomorrow.

'What doesn't open?'

The office supplies shop. I need some ink. I have a will to write.

'A will? Whose will?'

It makes your ear hot, this phone. Let's end the call.

I put the phone back in my pocket. I was a bit frightened of my daughter-in-law, even though it was she who ought to be frightened of me. My daughter-in-law eats vegetarian food and I saw on a documentary that Adolf Hitler also ate vegetarian food. It's my daughter-in-law who earns the money in their family and she can reverse the car into the tiniest parking space. I gave up thinking about things and headed for the sauna.

You could borrow swimming trunks from a basket. I took a pair with me and opened the glass door behind which were the shower room and the sauna.

I examined the glass door for a moment.

Glass is meant for windows. Why, nowadays, is it used for walls and doors? How do you attach hinges and a handle to glass? Glass breaks, after all, when the children decide to play ice hockey inside or an old person walks into a door. Then there are shards on the floor and a hole in the head.

Wood endures, use wood.

This is how it went: a rich American wanted to see through a door. A door was made. The ordinary and the sensible are not enough; things have to be extraordinary and senseless. What's wanted is sparkle, accessories and electrical gadgets. And why not, if these follies were restricted to a rich man's sauna or terrace, but now a rich man's whims are being mass produced in China so that even a poor person can afford a glass door. Little boys and girls make glass doors and can't go to school. There aren't any schools, only factories. How do I know? Because it was once like that in this country, too.

And soon the poor people of Finland will have
glass doors, massaging shower-heads and skin-care
products that promise eternal youth. But the poor
in Finland don't have jobs, they were gathered up
and moved to China. Among all their stuff the rich
and the poor sit in their identical saunas and mourn.
In their mirrored cupboards, beside the skin-care
products, is a pot of mind-medicines that are used
to fill the void, although an hour's cross-country
skiing would do the trick. But there's no snow.
It disappeared along with climate change. Which
developed when children in China started making
glass doors and chemical factories began producing
wonder creams and the factories started puffing
pollution into the sky without anyone tracking the
emissions or human rights. It's more important that
we here should be able to buy as many bad products
as possible, cheaply.

I had to stop to draw breath.

When my pulse had settled, I had one more thought
to add.

On the side of the skin-care package it says that the
product has been tested in a Swiss vitamin institute.
It also says that it has sixty-seven per cent more skin-
renewing ingredients.

I ask: more than what?!

Has anyone been to Switzerland to check that
there is a vitamin institute? Is there a sign in
Geneva that says, this way to the ice rink, this way
to the mountain that looks like the Toblerone packet,

and this way to the vitamin institute? I have my doubts.

I took a cold shower because the thoughts were burning my head. Or I would have done, but I was prevented from doing so. The shower had decided the temperature on my behalf. The knob did not move in any direction.

You can't decide anything for yourself, because the engineer designed it and automation has replaced the all-knowing God and, in the army, the bossy sergeant-major. Automation dictates in advance what our place is and where our path will lead us. Your shower can last only for a certain amount of time, the water is supposed to come out at a specified temperature and a soap dispenser deposits a certain amount into the palm of your hand. Your car beeps if you'd like, just this once, to drive without fastening your seat-belt. Your food is ready-packed, and soon it will be ready-chewed.

Nowadays I'm the one who seeks the exotic, because I want hard pillows, bars of soap and handles. If I want a cold shower, I have to call the hotel manager and I am sure it has been agreed somewhere in the Department of Health that you should wear a helmet. And a wetsuit if you're intending to shower in water of less than thirty degrees. Accident researchers and the United Nations will be taken by helicopter to work out what made an eighty-year-old man turn the shower a little colder. A special news report will announce that counselling has been arranged for local residents.

*

It's important to understand the danger of warm water.
It begins, after a moment in the shower, to feel good
and right. Water reserves and electricity are used up,
the skin softens, and the soul mellows. Your willpower
is washed down the drain along with the warm, soapy
water. Finnish children are becoming fatheads, as
Finnish adults already are.

'Press there, look, and then turn,' comes a voice from
somewhere.

The water cooled down.

I was slightly suspicious of the intervention, but I
had to say thank you. The helper was a boy of the age
when your skin is bad who would, in the old days,
have been in the prime of his working life; nowadays
he would be found on the school bench or on the sofa.
I took a twelve-second shower, which is enough time
for a person to refresh and clean themselves properly.

A step toward the sauna. The boy opened the door
and let me in. This was an unusually civilised youth.
I tested whether he could take the heat by throwing a
good seven ladlefuls of water on to the stove.

'Do you mind if I talk to you?' asked the youth when
the heat had dissipated and he was able to breathe
again.

I asked if he was a travelling salesperson. Had he
filled in 'leisure' or 'work' on the check-in form? Did
he understand that even though we were in a hotel the
same laws held as in real life, you can't just go to sleep
with your shoes on or party on into the small hours.

The civilised youth said he was a sixth-former and on a trip with his mother, who was on a business trip to this medium-sized Finnish town.

Your mother is a travelling salesperson?

'She's a lecturer.'

I often forget this. All these jobs that didn't used to exist. And ladies who live men's lives. They earn money in the world so that the men have time to infuse seeds in lukewarm water and ponder whether to drop the community college yoga course and take up recorder-playing.

'And what about you, if I may ask? What brought you here?'

I thought for a moment as to whether I should tell the truth or if it would be used against me. His eyes looked honest, so I revealed that I was on an ink-buying trip.

'For a printer?'

For a will.

'You need ink for a will? Is it a black-and-white printer, or a laser printer?'

Don't they teach what a will is at school?

'Are you going to die?'

Everyone dies.

'Do you have some illness?'

I haven't really had anything more than a couple of cases of the flu in my life, and each of them has gone just the same way as it came. By rolling in the snow. I asked whether the boy's father was soaking chickpeas.

'I think he's somewhere above Tibet at the moment.'

Was it a metaphor? I don't like that kind of talk. If you can say something straight, then you should do so.

'My father is on his way back from a work trip to South Korea. I'm going to stay with them for a couple of weeks when Dad comes back. He lives with my stepmother . . .'

I told the civilised youth that in the old days men took a lover as a substitute wife. You needed something like that when the intense interest in romping with your life partner began to fade. You shouldn't rush with things like that. Six years can go by when you concentrate on your own work and prefer to look at your own toenails rather than your wife's. Then, on some unpredictable day, your wife begins to look exactly the same as the first time you saw her.

Like the meaning of the world.

Then the Sixties arrived, and lovers became part of the general confusion. Red-wine drinkers, guitar-strummers, long-hair growers and people who made a noise about free love, they were all jumbled together. Garbled speech and scornful laughter made their appearance on television. Even the presenters of news documentaries were visibly drunk. And it's only got worse. There aren't any documentaries any more, only light entertainment.

'We've read about student radicalism at school.'

The family sure is a unit that you either start or you don't. My son and my daughter-in-law should understand that.

'I think it would be better for them.'

My son and my daughter-in-law?

'I don't know them. I mean my own parents.'

He sure was a bit on the cheeky side, this youth. I asked his opinion on the matter. Was it better to be at home or in an hotel somewhere far away?

The boy was unable to answer, but said he was going for a swim. I stayed in the sauna for a moment, and threw a half-ladleful on the stove so that I could feel it in my earlobes.

The Sixties led to the ladies going out to work and beginning to catch up with the men in all possible things. But instead of teaching the men their own good habits, they nabbed the bad ones from them. Put cigarettes between their lips, opened a cider bottle, began to take a look at neighbouring tables and families. Studied subjects that didn't lead to jobs. Began to pop contraceptive pills, so that, like men, they no longer had to think about who they went with to the bedroom, the birch wood or the loo at the young people's concert. And now ladies have permission, and almost the duty, to be interested in men younger themselves.

Is that what was happening with my daughter-in-law and my son?

The ladies have education, money and status, so that young men are interested in them. Older people use make-up and tell the surgeon to slice their chins and their mammary glands so that they look like girls of eighteen summers. They sure don't accept their own lives and situations, but yearn for other times. They want to go back, or to take a great leap forward.

Death is feared, life is mocked. I pulled the swimming trunks on and climbed down the swimming pool steps calmly, estimating the temperature of the water at twenty-five and a half degrees. That is ten too many. The civilised youth pulled an energetic backstroke as if his swimming could take him from this pool to somewhere else. When he came to the surface, I told him more about the vale of tears that is life.

Young people try to live it as if today is their last day, because they are afraid it will end tomorrow. They think life is short and therefore your bar bill should be long and your speed high. They try to live a decade in the course of a year. They experiment as to what it is like to be alone, together and in a group, study and have a gap year at the same time, travel on cheap airlines and by Interrail and move from Christianity to Buddhism by way of atheism and the Vikings' runestones because they are open to all kinds of nonsense. The only thing they aren't interested in is sensible talk.

The civilised youth came to the surface and drew breath for a moment. I brought up the rear with a peaceful breaststroke; it's a bit like pushing with both poles at the same time in skiing, only in swimming.

Yes, I correct myself, commenting: life is long.

When I turned forty, I knew that I had lived longer than my ancestors had on average. That is enough. The house was built, the mortgage paid off, the kids had moved away from home. If I had any dreams, I sure didn't voice them.

Everything, after those years, was a bonus.
I thought I would go on working until I was seventy-seven, after which I would sit at home with my wife and hold her hand. The grandfather clock would tick, we would watch television for a moment, we would leaf through newspapers and at Christmas we would ask each other who sent cards to us today and should we get a tree and is the ham properly defrosted.
I would look forward to the Four Hills Tournament and mark the first coltsfoot in my diary. Then we would die like an old pine tree. Perhaps three days apart, first me then my wife.

Then there was this being left alone.

I don't complain. I'm not in pain. And I'm not completely alone. Often it's just somehow pointless. As if you were sitting in the doctor's waiting room and your turn to see the doctor never comes. A person needs to have something more important to do than to sit looking out of the window at the same landscape where the only things to change are the leaves on the trees.

'I'm sorry, I didn't hear everything. I have to swim a kilometre every day.'

Have to?

'Playing the violin makes me stiff.'

That was an interesting piece of information. I could have a use for him. A proper funeral has proper music. Even though I don't dance or celebrate myself, there would be nothing to prevent the funeral party from doing so. If there were a skilful violinist on offer, then he could play my favourite piece.

'I will make a mental note of it.'

The civilised youth didn't come back into the sauna. I poured the rest of the water straight on to the stove and was ready to leave myself.

I was surprised when the young man was still in the dressing room, now with his clothes on and a television in his lap. He lifted the television and pressed something. There was a sound like a camera trigger.

'Can I post a picture of you on Instagram? Sorry . . . Your face won't be visible, and I won't give any personal details. But I think important meetings should be recorded.'

The civilised youth turned the television in my direction and there I stood, as if in a photograph.

'Haven't you seen a tablet before?'

It sure wasn't any kind of tablet. Nitro and Imodium are tablets. Lemsip is a powder.

'Would you like to hold it?' the civilised youth asked.

My daughter-in-law was the same with babies. Shoving my grandchildren into my lap, even though I was afraid I would drop them on the floor. I tried to hold the lap television as you would a gas cylinder, strongly, cautiously and confidently.

'What would you like to look at?'

I checked the time. The news was about to start.

'Which news?'

What do you mean?

'The five o'clock, the seven o'clock, the six o'clock? The local news?'

Can you choose?

'Of course.'

The Sámi news, then.

And in a moment we saw once again what was happening in the Sámi areas of northern Finland, Norway, Sweden and Russia, and a short report on sports competitions among local people. The one where they played polo with a lamb carcass sure was an interesting event. I began to be interested in whether you could use the device to see further away. Could you watch yesterday's news? Could you see last year's news. Could you even see the news read by Arvi Lind in 'Seventy-nine? Khomeini's rise to power? I could show it to the civilised youth. He touched the television screen and what looked like a typewriter keyboard made its appearance.

'Do you write this Lind with an "h"? Does it end with an "h"?'

Goodness gracious me. Lind. Arvi Lind.

'I don't ever watch Finnish television.'

A comforting picture appeared on the machine's screen: Arvi in a brown sports jacket and a black tie. Behind him was a picture of Leonid Brezhnev. We never got to start the news, because there was a knock on the dressing-room door. A woman's voice was calling my name. I wondered how anyone here knew it.

'Will you come! The food is getting cold! We're waiting!'

It was Margaret Thatcher. It was my daughter-in-law. I had to say goodbye to the civilised youth. I got some kind of electronic address from him; he hoped I would write him a letter or let him have my news. I sure didn't understand a word of what he said, but because he was the first representative of the younger generation to make sense since the year 1953, I gave him my postal address in return. He might send me a card or a letter, and if he happened to drive by, I'd make some coffee.

Live and let liver

Even if it were to rain lizards or Finland were to return
to the gold standard in long-distance running, you would
have to keep a straight face. It sure isn't good for a person
to show their astonishment. Expressions are like big
words, you should have recourse to them only in extreme
need. If you suddenly begin to exclaim over things, saying
they're lovely or darling, then what do you do when
you're confronted with something truly impressive? An
unpleasant silence descended between me and my wife in
the autumn of 'Sixty-nine when she asked me about some
dress of hers, saying isn't it lovely. I wasn't able to give
her the answer she wanted. I was honest; I said it looked
like a slightly uncomfortable garment which would
shrink in the wash. She didn't like it; in the evening when
she was washing up, the dishes clattered.

I sure wondered how my daughter-in-law had
managed to find me in the sauna, but as she didn't say
I didn't ask her. Instead I enquired about the drive and
whether she was still driving that French jalopy, even
though it was at the top of all the lists of unreliable
vehicles. Had she put her winter tyres on? I hoped
she'd bought anti-skid tyres and not the sort of chains
that mean that you can't hear it's winter; it feels as if
you're on a midsummer drive.

My daughter-in-law said nothing.

Her mouth was certainly moving, but I couldn't hear
anything.

Water had probably got in my ear while I was
swimming, since I hadn't been able to hear at all with
my less good ear for a couple of years. I tried to hop
on one leg to clear it. I gave up because you can't do
that kind of bouncing in the same lift as my daughter-
in-law. What if the lift stopped and the door opened?
The hotel guests would think that an old man had been
hired as an entertainer and that soon he would start
to look them cheekily in the eye and engage them in
conversation.

I decided to keep the water in my ear and nodded at
my daughter-in-law as if I could hear everything. The
lift stopped at the lowest floor, where my daughter-in-
law pulled me after her into the hotel restaurant.

My son was sitting at the table staring at the glass
in front of him. He was turning it round, lifting

it into the air and holding it up against the light. He had always been like that, paying attention to strange things. When I tried to teach him how to drive a tractor as a child, he stood at the edge of the field wondering whether migratory birds are called migratory birds in Africa too. Do they have to migrate all the time and where is their real home? I grunted at him to focus on the steering wheel, but that evening I wondered whether an Arctic tern goes by the same name on the other side of the world. How do they find their way? It took human beings tens of thousands of years to discover all the continents and they still got places muddled up. Migratory birds sure must have followed Columbus's wanderings with a smile at the corner of their beaks and as they discussed how to get to the next place that popped into their tiny brains.

I'd not eaten since breakfast, so a basket of chicken or sausage was going to be very welcome. I examined the menu, on which everything was expensive. I chose what I've always chosen on each of the seven occasions when I have been to a restaurant.

I left the menu in front of me so that I could watch my son and my daughter-in-law.

There were some half-filled glasses on the table. My daughter-in-law gulped hers before I had even sat down. My son snatched the glass away from her. They said something to one another; I did not hear what. I took a napkin and tried to excavate my ear with it. My son spoke directly to me and I replied that my ears were blocked. My son shook his head and snorted, at me or else at the world.

They didn't look at each other once, glancing sideways and avoiding one another's gaze instead. My son was stiff and clumsy, my daughter-in-law apparently ready to attack in some direction. From time to time one of them tried to catch the other's eye, but then the other one would look away. It reminded me of my wife and me. At times there were moments and years when suddenly the other one would seem like more of a stranger than before. The same thing which had yesterday caused a pleasant tickle in the chest was just boring and repetitive.

My daughter-in-law's mouth was moving and I tried to listen. The bubble must have got a bit smaller because some words stuck to my ear.

' . . . how can you . . .?'

Did my son have some illness?

' . . . you can't . . .'

My son muttered an answer which I didn't catch. Arguing sure is pointless but people do it all the same. At this age you don't want to be in the middle of a row so I never watch election debates on the television any more. All they do is quarrel, speak in high-pitched voices and blame each other, while not pursuing what should be the purpose of democracy: make good decisions. They are not exactly difficult matters: the care of the elderly, the standard of primary schools and the sustainability gap. They must be seen to and everyone must participate. Take a collection and do volunteer work; don't harp on about what you did in the last electoral term. It sure is clear from the Middle East what happens when you continually remember the past.

I've offered my advice to the government, but I didn't get an answer to my postcard. This is what it said:

> Everyone wants tomorrow to be better than today. That's wrong. How much better it would be if we decided that yesterday was better than tomorrow. We wouldn't demand new things but would realise that this is enough. This food, these public services and this car, 1973 model. Ordinary things are enough.

But nations and men and women have to quarrel. The closer the person, the uglier it gets. Energy is wasted; things that matter to everyone are set against each other when they should go side by side. Or they should be put in the same pot. I could never bear to quarrel with my wife for long; generally it didn't last longer than a year. My quarrel with Kolehmainen is, I think, in its sixteenth year.

I heard some more words from here and there.

'We can't keep it any longer . . .'

'What do you mean we can't, of course we can . . .'

They were negotiating hard about something.

If you don't know something and there is uncertainty, one thing always helps. A night's sleep. The mind of someone who was in despair yesterday can be brisk and bright in the morning, with the next step clear. They listened to me when I gave them an example from my own life. In the late autumn of 'Eighty-nine the Ford Escort wouldn't start. I was afraid I would have to call the tow-truck, which would cost many hundred Finnish marks.

In the morning the matter was as clear as a child's forehead. The petrol pipe had rusted and had to be replaced. I don't know why I hadn't realised straight away. The part cost nine and a half Finnish marks at Hukkonen's. On the radio I heard that the Berlin Wall had come down.

My daughter-in-law said something, but I hadn't finished.

In addition to a night's sleep, another thing that can help is setting a difficult matter aside. When, in 'Thirty-nine, call-ups for extra military refresher courses were issued, the wisest people simply continued their lives as they had done until then. They did their work, looked after their families and set off when it was time. Stupider folk drank their hidden booze, ruining the lives they were going to the frontier to defend and lose. On the other hand it tended to be the drinkers who came back on their own two feet, while the better men made their way home in wooden coffins. Were they so crooked that they dodged the bullets?

Somehow this latter example of mine cooled the atmosphere, and my daughter-in-law poured herself some more wine. My son tried to take the glass away. When he did not succeed, he poured mineral water on top of the wine.

The waiteress came up with her notebook, making small-talk, but I didn't hear what she said. My daughter-in-law waved her hand and showed her credit card. She wanted to pay in advance; apparently she was in a hurry.

I wanted to pay. And I wanted some buttermilk.

My son scratched his arm. He's always scratched his arms when he's stressed. In ski competitions, just before the off, he would often take his poles and his gloves off and scratch. I nodded at his arm. He understood what I meant immediately.

There was a long, awkward silence during which my daughter-in-law folded the napkin in her lap, as did my son. I said I was capable of eating without making a mess and left the napkin where it was. The food took a long time to arrive, and I said I would send them my will to read, once I had got some ink. They were not allowed to interfere with the content, but with spellings, grammar and layout certainly.

The food came after a long wait and my ear stayed blocked. On my daughter-in-law's plate was some dwarf cabbage and she knew what to do with it, how to sprinkle wine vinegar on it and then mix it up. My son began to spoon up his soup at once.

There was a pile of red onion on top of my liver. In the old days there was only one kind of onion, the kind you dug up from the fields. Now there was a whole wall of them hanging in the shop, and if you invented a new colour you could charge twice the price.

As I swallowed the buttermilk I heard a little crackle and then I felt a strange itch. I began to be able to make out sounds, the clink of glasses, a child's whingeing. I could also hear my daughter-in-law's words quite clearly . . .

'We can't have another child . . .'

I put the pile of onion in my mouth and popped in a piece of liver after it. I said I could hear again. My daughter-in-law turned to me.

'We can't keep the child!'

Why can't you have one?

'I'm over forty. I'm don't want to have any more sleepless nights!'

I turned to look at my son. Now I understood that this was the reason he was crying tears of happiness and sadness at the same time. They'd learned to combine the two, the men of today. In the old days you had to be able to ski jump and then ski downhill afterwards. Or reverse a car and smoke a cigarette. Or keep the children at arm's length and slaughter a pig.

'We'll keep it,' my son said.

'It's your decision, then?'

I put some liver in my mouth. I drank some buttermilk from a mug that was empty. I waved it at the waitress like people with a great thirst for alcohol do in the movies.

It was a pity that my hearing had come back. I rolled up little plugs out of paper and pushed them into my ears. There are things I shouldn't hear.

'I just can't do broken nights,' I heard through the plugs.

'I can,' my son answered.

I sure don't understand why anyone can't do broken nights. I'm more surprised that people can stay up at night.

'Is it you who's going to carry the baby, then?' my daughter-in-law asked my son.

'All you need to do is give birth.'

'What?' my daughter-in-law snapped, holding her knife so that I thought she was going to stab my son. I asked for the salt so she would have to set the knife down. I asked if there was any reason for us to be in such a bad mood. Why do people cry about a new life when there's no sense in weeping over death?

'Don't try to be smart, old man.'

Someone's got to be the old man when everyone else is being childish. There was an awkward silence from my daughter-in-law. She folded her napkin up in her lap and got up. Placed her hand on my shoulder.

'I'm not really thinking straight. I mean. I think it's better if we leave . . .'

Then they were gone. I watched through the restaurant window as they got into the car, argued for a moment about who was going to drive and then left. The waitress came to ask whether the food had been good and I said it didn't matter whether it had been good or not, we'd eaten it. Mine, my daughter-in-law's and my son's. Happy days to you too.

I went straight to bed, but the red dot kept me awake. Why is it that electronic devices are kept unnecessarily on standby? How many rooms are there in the hotel, how many televisions? Four hundred and sixteen. For that reason new nuclear power stations have to be planned and then there are arguments about whether they should be built because there'll be a tsunami which will destroy good people's homes and lives. Why can't a television just have an off button? Why doesn't anything have an off button?

Although I was upset, I was at the breakfast restaurant's door in good time.

I have my doubts as to whether anyone needs peppers, scrambled eggs, boiled eggs, white bread, seeded bread, jams, gravadlax, salami, pancakes, whipped cream, fish roe, children's cereals, twenty different types of tea and seven juices for breakfast.

Naturally I tasted everything, since it was free.

Mould works surprisingly well on cheese. Much better than on bread or in the basement of your house. I couldn't eat everything, so I wrapped it up in my napkin and put it in my pocket. I thought I would take it to my wife and Anneli as a present.

I drank a good number of cups of coffee, as you never know when you will get your next one. That was a habit from wartime, when the gap between coffee-breaks stretched to a little over four years.

I walked from the hotel to the office supplies shop – I'd made a note of its location the previous day – and took a bottle of ink from the shelf. I also asked for eight sheets of the best paper.

I returned to the hotel desk and began to write. I took the ink bottle from its little paper bag, dipped my pen in the ink; it was viscous and liquid in just the right way. The young sure don't know what they're missing out on when they write on their smartphones. They lose contact.

I took the sheets of paper from the envelope and put one on the table. I got into a comfortable position and waited a moment for my breathing to settle down, like a ski biathlete before a perfect performance. I sure do believe that Heikki Ikonen's will is written with a steady hand.

I . . .

That's what I should have written. But it looked more like a 'U' or a 'J'.

The ink spread and the letters broke up as if a child had been on the job. I was really upset when my will turned into a modernist work of art. It wasn't stress or because I was shaking due to the cold, but nerves. I've noticed it in the workshop, but when you're using the plane or the saw you can control your shaking by tying your forearm into place with a piece of string. Or by supporting it against the workbench.

I took a new piece of paper and concentrated. I pressed my wrist against the desk and ordered my hand to stay in place. The result looked even more like a wall painting by some young person or stone-age idiot. I was sorry that I hadn't agreed to the cortisone injection Kivinkinen had recommended; instead I'd explained to him that skiers get shots and the janitor had injected the long-distance runner Martti Vainio in a doping scandal and it was a good thing that the paediatrician Arvo Ylppö had had the idea of vaccinating the little ones. But no one was going to come near me with a needle on account of little aches and pains.

The whole trip with my son had been fruitless. Now I knew things I'd have preferred not to know and had paid seven euros for some ink which would just dry up alongside the old bottle. Because of my vexation my hand shook even more than before and I decided to forget all about my will for a moment, just like I forgot about the cross-country skier Juha Mieto's hundredth-second defeat in 1980. Sometimes you just have to accept the facts.

At this age you can't rebel any more. I thought: this hand will get better, just like my old Salora television with its wooden case, which lost its picture in the spring of 'Eighty-six. I took it up to the attic and I believe that when I bring it down one day it will work again.

Like a bed of roses

Back at home, I put the Escort in the garage and went to the workshop. I lifted the box of photographs out of the cupboard and noticed a plastic pocket on the floor. In it I had stored my only friend Yrjänä's death notice, his will, the book of condolences and photographs. In the photogaphs Yrjänä lay in an open coffin; the reflection of the flash gleamed on his forehead and he no longer looked anything like himself. I tried to bring the funeral to mind, but for some reason I could recall no smell or sound. We ate Karelian hotpot, or did we? Were the heirs trying to be unusual by serving cold food? In the photographs Yrjänä was wearing a black suit as if he were setting off on an important business trip.

A man sure should have a proper suit for his own funeral.

I went up to the attic.

My wedding suit was in its place on a wooden hanger, beside my wife's wedding dress. I tried to pull the sleeves down and stand in a slightly different position, but then I looked like a member of parliament forced to be satisfied with eight votes. If your coffin is designed to your own measurements your suit should also be a good fit.

The solution presented itself as I looked out of the little attic window. I could see over the tops of the birches and spruces to Kolehmainen's garden, in which something strange was going on. Their house had been quiet for a long time; they had probably been on a trip to his wife's homeland.

Kolehmainen was reaching up into the air with both hands in a strange way. I noticed that he was about my size, except for his belly, which has filled out a lot. Maybe Kolehmainen could lend me one of his many suits. I remember how often he had bragged about how cheaply you can things made by a tailor in Thailand.

I put on my boots and my fur hat.

I took a shortcut under the power line and was able to surprise Kolehmainen from behind. He was still stretching out his arms in the garden and I had to peer at him for a long time before I made out that there was a fishing line in his hand. At the end of the line something was moving.

I tapped on his shoulder. Kolehmainen started as if he'd seen a ghost.

His hands stopped moving. A colourful kite floated to the ground. I asked why a grown man was flying a kite.

'You never know with these things, you have to try them out. It got a bit crushed in the aeroplane; I had to glue it together. What can I do for you?'

I said not a word about the lawnmower, the plane, the jump-leads or even the sack of flour that my dad lent his dad in 'Forty-eight. I said I wanted to buy a suit from him.

'What kind of suit do you mean?'

A black suit.

'Who for?'

Who else would I buy a black suit for but myself?

'Why on earth?'

I suggested we go inside to continue the conversation; I needed the help of Kolehmainen's wife for this. Kolehmainen wound the line round a reel and stamped his boots a couple of times on the outside steps. The door opened before we could touch the handle. Kolehmainen's wife's radiantly smiling face came into view.

'Welcome!'

I put out my hand to stop the lady from coming too close. She evidently felt the same resistance, because she bowed and took a step backwards. I value such things greatly. I sure do understand a dog's territory because it will bite you or pee on your feet if the wrong person tries to enter, but a human is supposed to be prepared to embrace unknown people or slobber over them with a kiss on the cheek.

I came straight to the point. A black suit, a good price, no need for any room for growth. Kolehmainen gave me an appraising glance, but his wife fetched a tape measure from on top of the cupboard in the hall.

'Is it for a confirmation?'

No.

'A wedding?'

No.

'A funeral?'

I nodded.

Kolehmainen and his wife said they were sorry for my loss. Kolehmainen asked who had died, hopefully not my own wife. I said it would become clear to them, they sure would be getting an invitation. The main thing was that I needed the suit and I would be most grateful if they could supply one. Kolehmainen's wife said she would be happy to. She remembered very well how I had lent them two blue buckets and one red one for the berry forest and, last winter, helped her to climb the highest hill on the ski trail. Where she came from they always helped their neighbours. I told her that that's what they did where I came from too, in the Fifties. I was astonished that Kolehmainen himself did not help his wife. Why didn't he show her how to do a herringbone walk; he had just sent her out alone to ski. Although it's true that you learn best when you're alone, confronted by necessity and death. I myself learned to swim when my father dropped me out of the boat.

I was the one who showed the Thai lady how to let the pole swing casually round to the back and kick sharply. If you're on a long trip you can slide along, saving energy. I was tempted to ask if Kolehmainen would be able to learn how to drive a three-wheeled moped through the rush hour in Thailand. I have my doubts. But Kolehmainen's wife skied down handsomely in egg position like the Olympic cross-country skier Helena Takalo and didn't go into snowplough until the very end. And she even skied down a slope that my wife would prefer to walk.

I believe that, from a young age, people from Thailand have to crouch in the rice paddies and the berry forests; they don't sit in soft chairs fingering screens and thinking about what depresses them most today. The past or the future. Loneliness or teamwork. Picking rice develops precisely the same muscles as are useful in skiing downhill; for this reason the next leading cross-country ski nation will be China.

As I was thinking this, Kolehmainen's wife disappeared to look for the suit and I sat with Kolehmainen at their table. I could hear cupboards opening and closing upstairs. I looked at Kolehmainen, who was looking out of the window. My wife always wondered what it was that made things between him and me so difficult. She wanted to know what I was really whingeing about, why he always just seemed to annoy me so much. But I sure don't remember where it all started.

Now I was having to think about those I would leave behind. I was having to think about the consequences of a quarrel with a neighbour. If my home were to become a summer-place for my grandchildren, it would be necessary to have cordial relations with the neighbours. You need them for clearing snow in the winter or for scaring burglars away.

'She makes them herself these days,' Kolehmainen said. 'Suits. Good with her hands. Yes. We import the fabric from Thailand and sew them here, to order. My wife does. Suits, shirts, trousers. Even a couple of dresses.'

I nodded.

'The taxman be damned,' Kolehmainen continued. 'All sorts of papers and fees and taxes and customs documents.'

I nodded. Kolehmainen lifted a coffee pot on to the table and dripped us a couple of cupfuls. It was easier once the cups and coffee were between us. Kolehmainen surmised that once they'd dealt with the red tape they would have a good business. I said we didn't need to do business. I need the suit for one single day, I could pay in services rendered or in potatoes.

I tasted my coffee.

Suddenly a small boy appeared in the room.

He had been playing quietly somewhere else, but now he stood before us with a serious expression on his face. He looked more like Kolehmainen's wife than Kolehmainen himself. I asked whether Kolehmainen knew the child.

'Jarmo,' Kolehmainen said.

'Jalmo,' the boy said.

'Shake our neighbour's hand.'

Kolehmainen explained that the boy's real name had been difficult for him. Jarmo is good. I estimated Jarmo to be about five years old. On the school-bus run I have learned to distinguish between those who are of kindergarten age and those who are schoolchildren, but I'm aided in defining their ages by their style of backpack, woolly hats and friends. The number of teeth or gaps also helps. The same is true of old people.

The boy sat on Kolehmainen's lap and pushed a toy car across the table. He made the same noises as a Finnish toy car makes when played with by a Finnish boy. I sure was glad of the arrival of a third person in addition to me and Kolehmainen, so that I didn't have to think too hard about all the things I should leave unsaid.

'We finally managed to have Jarmo join us,' Kolehmainen told me.

Where from?

'From his old home country. This is his home country now.'

Jarmo had lived with his grandmother from the time when Kolehmainen's wife moved in with Kolehmainen. There had been red tape – that form 'C' and 'D' with form 'A' and all its appendices should be collated was apparently more important than that a mother and son be reunited. Such things were familiar to me now that I had checked into a twenty-first century hotel.

'He certainly misses his grandmother,' Kolehmainen said. 'But I think he wants to be here with his mother even more.'

That's the kind of thing a person finds themselves having to work out and weigh up during their lives. I sure didn't always want to go to the building site; I would have preferred to stay with the family at the breakfast table, but work is work and you got used to the routine. You just had to remember that it wasn't home.

I asked whether Kolehmainen had flown the kite for Jarmo; was it Jarmo's kite? Kolehmainen conceded that it's best to have familiar toys when you've changed country. They would make the change to more traditionally Finnish toys later, like air guns and quad bikes.

I had never seen Kolehmainen like this before, caring about anyone other than himself.

I counted the months in my head and recalled their events. I had my doubts as to whether Kolehmainen could be the boy's father.

'Let's not make an easy thing harder,' Kolehmainen said as if he could read my thoughts. 'Jarmo needs a father. I need a son. Jarmo will carry the business on.'

I felt like asking where, because Kolehmainen's fields had been fallow since Seppo Räty won the world championship. They had no animals apart from their hunting dog. But it seemed a fine thing. My grandchildren and their children could play with Jarmo's children someday. Then there could be a row of kites above our village. Maybe the school would even reopen.

I asked whether the boy drank coffee. Kolehmainen said people from Thailand were more tea people, but he had learned to dunk his cardamom *pulla* buns. The boy left off his game for a moment and got out of Kolehmainen's lap. He had understood what we said and opened the pantry door.

'Coffeecoffeecoffee. *Pullapullapulla.*'

The boy brought us some *pulla* and cut some good, for his age extraordinarily straight slices. He brought a pack of butter. Kolehmainen buttered his own slice. I asked him whether he still ate frankfurters with his *pulla*.

'I have diabetes too. Have to watch what I put in my mouth. If it gets worse I'll get my own shots in the thigh.'

I showed the boy how to pull your thumb off the palm of your hand. It was a trick I learned as a young man from my mates in the army barracks. The boy responded by pulling his eyelids down and puffing his cheeks. Kolehmainen's wife came into the kitchen at the point when I was making my nose into a pig's snout and the boy was copying me.

In her arms she had a pile of multicoloured clothes. She said something about *pulla* and opened the chest freezer. I realised we had eaten in the wrong order. First savoury, then sweet.

Kolehmainen's wife took some icy chunks of moose meat out of the freezer, found what she was looking for and replaced the chunks. I reflected that the coffin I had made for myself would fit in its entirety into Kolehmainen's freezer. Kolehmainen sure would be surprised if he found me when rummaging for cheesecake for a late-night snack.

Kolehmainen's wife said something in her own language to Jarmo, who got off his chair again and looked in the crockery cupboard for various mugs and saucepans. He knew how to turn on the electric hob, and set a frying pan on it. He defrosted the food for a moment in the microwave and then clunked it on to the bottom of the pan. At the same time Kolehmainen's wife opened the bag of clothes.

She asked me to stand up and held a grey suit against me. Took my hand in hers and ran my fingers over the material. It certainly was soft, like another person's skin.

Kolehmainen said that his wife wanted me to go for a fitting. I think it's wrong that people strip down to their underclothes behind the curtain in a fitting room. There are bound to be some of those American-invented X-ray glasses that see through the curtain and anyway, how can you see what a garment looks like or how it fits in such a small space? You only know that when you've worn it for a year at work, in your free time and when you've got a flat tyre on a dark forest road, but will any shopkeeper agree to lending you clothes for those purposes?

My wife used to like going to try things on in the big department store in the city, even though she had no intention of buying anything. While she was doing it I'd be reading the contents of oil and lubrication cans in the motor department. Why did they have to be written in so many languages? There is 'Fin' and 'Est' and 'Swe' and 'Rus' and 'S' by itself and 'D' by itself and the same information every time. I suggested Latin as an operational language. I don't know Latin – there were boys from different farms who went to the grammar school – but I sure would learn if the milk carton said, time after time, in Latin, how many preservatives, how much protein and how much fat it contained.

You can't refuse the request of someone's wife in her own house. She directed me to the sauna dressing room and put one suit in my arms, hanging another on a peg. Kolehmainen, too, had installed underfloor heating and got those vibrating toothbrushes, because change comes along with wives. At our house it meant an indoor toilet and lined shelves in the kitchen cupboards. And Christmas lights in rooms even if there is nobody in them.

I don't know what the world would be like without wives. Presumably men would have working cars and good work shoes, but would anyone clean the windows? Would the carpet be changed because the colour had gone out of fashion? Would the dishwasher have been invented, or would one wooden spoon be enough for the whole of mankind? Would anyone wash their hands?

The suit felt as light as air. I wondered how good the Thais' work clothes must be. Protective, cool, but not tight anywhere. I'm sure nothing like that has been invented for the Finnish climate yet. I had to check in the mirror that I had actually put any clothes on.

I didn't dare leave the dressing room to show myself, but waited for Kolehmainen's wife to knock on the door and ask if I wanted to try anything else on.

The first is always the best. I said I would take the suit and asked how much I owed them. Kolehmainen called out from the kitchen that a hundred would do. His wife shook her head. She wanted to give the suit to me to say thank you for the ski-teaching and the good neighbourliness. Plus three berry pies from the freezer.

The boy Jarmo had laid the table with plates and cutlery. Chopsticks for the others, and for me a knife and fork. Although I felt that after such a generous deal I should respect the family and use chopsticks. To begin with they were hard to eat with, but then I had the idea of taking my knife from my belt and sharpening them. This way I was able to sink the point into the vegetables and the strips of meat. Kolehmainen's wife approved of this; she was quite amused.

Jarmo ate with a good appetite, even the beansprouts, which for my own grandchildren are always the most challenging element of a fish soup. Along with the potatoes, the pieces of fish and the milky stock. I willingly ate the rice with a spoon and I noticed that Jarmo, too, wanted to try the spoon. He didn't yet dare, but perhaps when he was alone in the evening.

Kolehmainen's wife provided more than I was used to. Generally there are potatoes and a sauce. Here there was one dish after another, and all sorts of colours in those dishes. The white wasn't cow's milk but coconut milk. The green was not poison but curry. Her curry had a good, strong flavour. It tasted good; it sure is more pleasant to eat in company.

Kolehmainen's wife told all sorts of stories which I didn't understand very much. But she was able to demonstrate with her hands that she had found a good berry spot even after the first frosts. She explained that the boy had the fastest fingers of all, even if half the bilberries went straight into his mouth. That he should learn to ski and that I could help with this.

I said I would help if I was still here when the snow came. Kolehmainen asked me if I was going to move into the new sheltered accommodation in town; did I know what monthly rent they were asking? I said I knew well and didn't see any chance that I would be going there.

For pudding, Kolehmainen's wife served a really peculiar combination of a banana in some kind of pastry case with chocolate on top. A person sure would begin to put on a lot of weight if he ate such things every day, but once in a lifetime could hardly be dangerous. I wrapped the last third in paper and saved it for a more important occasion. When we had eaten everything Kolehmainen's wife wanted to say something. She took Jarmo in her arms and said that the most important thing was to have the boy here with her.

I nodded and I understood.

My wife sometimes talked about her neighbour Reija, who had been evacuated to Sweden in the war. She'd come back as a completely different little girl. Spoke strange Finnish and never really belonged anywhere her whole life. You don't always understand things like that when you have walked the same earth all your life.

Kolehmainen's wife hid her tears in the boy's hair and he thought she was tickling him. He giggled and wriggled and in this way, this slightly awkward and terribly beautiful situation happily came to an end.

I felt it was strange how easy it was to be with them, at home with my obnoxious neighbour. I still didn't get to go home because Jarmo wanted to fetch me a car of my own. A blue-and-white police car, bigger than his own, which made a noise when you pressed its siren. We drove the cars on the dining table, avoiding obstacles, which were the rice dish and the chicken dish and the buttermilk carton and the coffee pot.

It occurred to me that in the part of the world where Kolehmainen's wife and Jarmo were born there had been a bad storm that had swept entire villages into the sea. Perhaps that was why she smiled all the time. If you just dwell on the worst things in life and grieve over them, you won't have time for anything else. Of course you can build houses, as I, Yrjänä and the others did in our day. When something has been completely destroyed, there is enough work in mending the old and building the new to last for years. There is a meaning to life: you need to find shelter for the children, a bed for the old folk, some money for yourself and grateful looks from your nearest and dearest. Always there will be someone to cook hotpot and make coffee.

Kolehmainen's wife's folk survived their own upheavals just as we did here. But the same things can happen there as here. The standard of living rises, there are fewer necessary tasks, you have notes in your wallet, talking nonsense increases. Then you begin looking aimlessly out of the window and in the mirror. You go to places built by other people. You eat food prepared by other people. You buy machines for yourself instead of mending or knitting for others. This is the cause of all the illnesses which are not naturally part of people.

Obesity, depression, overdrafts, arrogance.

But when nature is angry, then man is small. If Storm Jorma were to tear the roof off my house or throw the Escort four kilometres or to hurl tree trunks over the garden wall, then I would have to resort to Kolehmainen. And he to me.

I offered Kolehmainen my hand and said we were now even. I promised always to make coffee for Jarmo and his wife. Potatoes, gravy and the sauna are on Saturdays at five o'clock. Kolehmainen wondered how we could ever have owed each other anything in the first place. I didn't begin to explain the past sixteen years, but grabbed Jarmo's police car again and drove it along the window for a moment instead.

Jarmo asked if I could be his Finnish grandpa. What could you say to that? To a five-year-old's request?

His home was a long way away. His new home was here because out of everyone in the world, Kolehmainen's wife had chosen Kolehmainen. You can't always understand things; generally you just have to marvel at them, like how Anita Hirvonen was at one time the nation's favourite singer.

I asked Kolehmainen's wife to tell her son that I couldn't be his grandpa, but I could be the old man next door. Or the old codger.

'Codger,' the boy repeated after me, pronouncing the word correctly.

We shook hands on it and it felt very good to be this boy's old man/codger. Now I had a godson next door just as my son and my daughter-in-law did somewhere in the Philippines. These days, when grown-ups are more and more often children, the more need there is for sense. I sure could be that for Jarmo. A bit like the oak tree in our garden. Always standing, never falling.

Eskimo turn

Dr Kivinkinen was interested in why I had changed
my mind about cortisone when I went into the surgery.
I said I needed a working hand in order to be able to
sign my will.

'An acceptable explanation,' Kivinkinen said,
sticking a needle in to the sore part.

It sure did remove the pain and the shaking, but at
the same time I lost sensation in my hand. I took a pen
and a piece of paper from the doctor's table and tried
to write. It was more awkward than before, since
I didn't know whether to hold my hand up or down,
or whether there was a pen in it at all.

'A temporary numbness,' Kivinkinen explained.
'It won't be an inconvenience or a pain for ever.'

You sure should to be able to distinguish between ailments and pain.

'And what's the difference, in your opinion?'

The difference is clear.

I began to have ailments when I turned forty-two. Before that I just grew, understanding and managing better each day than the one before. My knee snapped while I was climbing up onto the tin roof to mend a nail-hole. And it never got better. My back pains began to feel more like an attribute than a malfunction. Once on the building site a piece of concrete fell on my head, but luckily I was wearing a helmet. It broke and there was a lot of blood, but I was back at work the next week. It made me think that I don't much like pre-fabricated building, though.

I can live with my ailments; pain I would rather avoid. If, in the last metres of my life, I don't die with my boots on after all, but end up in a hospital bed, I will say: don't prolong my life unnecessarily. It's pointless treating any kind of ailment that you can't treat by gritting your teeth or lying on frosty ground. I would rather take the needle than spend years dribbling and bedridden.

'From a doctor's point of view it's not so simple.'

Whose life are we talking about? A person sure should be able to make the decisions about their own life.

'Well, I mean . . .' Kivinkinen mumbled.

The solution is simple, practical and wise from the point of view of the national economy. Everyone should have a comfort syringe in a locked cupboard in their own home. But no key. This would remove the risk of the syringe being used for frivolous reasons. Keys should be held by three friends and/or relatives who, together with the person in question, would decide when the ending of pain was a more humane option than the artificial prolongation of life.

'My personal opinion is really very close to what you're talking about,' Kivinkinen said. 'But it can only progress via legislation. We need a parliamentary bill . . .'

I promised to write a parliamentary bill as soon as my hand would let me.

Kivinkinen said I should take it easy for the rest of the day to allow the medicine to take effect. I said at this stage I sure was very well acquainted with my own capabilities and limitations, but hoped he would remember our conversation when I was near the final frontier.

At home I put on my silk suit. Because if I were to appear at the doctor's reception or in public in a black suit the blokes would think I'd won the lottery, even though I've never played the numbers games. Even the stupidest person knows that you can't win them. And if your ticket did win, why does a person need a million or seven? Why do you need a bigger house, a better car or a round-the-world trip? In eighty years I certainly haven't even seen all of the next parish. A suitable prize would be three packets of coffee or a tank of petrol.

I went to the workshop. I took my jacket off and rolled up the sleeves of my silk shirt. The cortisone hand moved a bit; I was able to use my left hand to tighten three screws until they were almost tight. I installed a lock on my coffin, too, because somehow it seemed like a good idea that the door should be locked even when you're underground pushing up the daisies. I added oil to the hinges and blew away the sawdust from the surfaces I'd planed.

I put a towel over the paintpot and sat down. I raised my hands into the air and stretched my legs. The Thai suit didn't strain at any point.

I understood why politicians and television Mafiosi have expensive suits. They have to stand under bright lights or in hot and smoky rooms all day; naturally that is easier in silk than in homespun clothes.

I wondered whether there was anything missing from the coffin; could I make it so that it had a special quality? Did my coffin need a mistake to customise it for me? Should I set it on runners so that in the winter it would slide smoothly behind a horse or a tractor?

I pulled a wooden stool under the workbench as a step. It was unsteady, but with the help of the chair and the workbench I was able to get into the coffin. I entered it as you get into a kayak, like the one Yrjänä once went and bought for no good reason. He was in the habit of making random purchases, just like the ladies do. He even bought a bread-making machine, the year that Jouko Kajander was a presidential candidate.

He used it three times.

The machine made bread that was tasty two and a half minutes after cooking. That is not a long time, if you consider that the sourdough rye loaves my wife used to make stays tasty for two and a half years after it's baked. You could have made good tennis balls with Yrjänä's machine's bread: the players could have eaten them between the second and third set instead of necking those fattening sports drinks or eating bananas.

First, I set my backside on the base of the coffin.

Then I straightened my legs in front of me and put my head on the pillow. The silk suit was smooth against the velvet of the coffin.

You can see from the ceiling that it was painted by the boys as a summer job. At some points there were large drips which had started to fall but had congealed.

I tried the inner surface of the coffin with the hand that obeyed my will. It still needed sanding, and it really should to be varnished on the inside too.

I decided to recommend coffin-building to my neighbour Jarmo as a sideline to farming. It would combine young people's skills in selling and inventing needs with the professional skills of able-bodied old men and women like me who had left the workforce. There are many competent pensioners in the country whose lives are lacking in purpose, work and companionship. The young people could deliver hand-made coffins to their customers and advertise them on their computer networks.

I had done such good work that I began to be tired. These days I feel sleepy at all the wrong times and so my eyes happened to close.

I don't know how long I was there, but I woke up to hear someone shouting my name in the garden. I was worried that it might be the home help or Dr Kivinkinen, and if they found me lying in a coffin in a black suit they wouldn't send me to a care home but to a home for the mentally ill.

I used my left hand to put my right on the edge of the coffin. Then I set the other hand down next to it. But when I raised my foot over the edge, my balance gave way completely, and being one-handed I couldn't control it.

What happened was the same as with Yrjänä's canoe that time.

An Eskimo turn.

I went down head first. That time into the water, this time on to concrete.

I was absolutely sure I was going to die.

And soon they're thirty

I blinked my eyes, lights flashed and I could hear the knocking of a diesel motor. We were moving fast in some direction and I was lying completely still on my back.

I was no longer in the coffin, but there was a strap across my chest. Did they think I would run away? Who thought so, and why?

Above me I could see a young man in a white coat and the face of some woman. It was my wife's face, or maybe not. It was my daughter-in-law's face, or maybe not.

All sorts of thoughts came into my head, one after the other.

I'd liked it when the children were born, at a time when the older folk were dying. Mother, father, uncle, cousin, the former president Juho Kusti Paasikivi,

Reino Lämsä, Jonteri Kussila or was it Aaretti and many others.

When you sat and gazed at the life of a snuffling one-day-old, it just felt good. Even more I liked how much my wife liked our offspring. She worked out who looked like whom, whether they looked like the family or just like themselves.

I remember the children crawling across the cabin floor and the sun streaming in.

I remember how they cried and wailed and learned to say important words. It was good to think that they could learn all the things that I hadn't been able to study.

I hadn't been able to finish school, but maybe my children would. If I hadn't ever been able to ride a pig, maybe my offspring would have the opportunity.

Mummy, cow, log-carving.

Those were the children's first words. Or was I repeating them as I lay there, were they my last words? Were a beginning and an ending merrily mixing themselves up?

Car, Daddy, potato.

Tayto, as one of them said.

The white-coated young man's face disappeared from in front of me. My daughter-in-law or my wife told me everything was fine. I shouldn't worry, I needed to stay calm, just lie there. I wasn't thinking straight and for a moment I didn't know what time I was in.

These days everything is easier than it was before. For that reason many things go badly, but there are some that go better. For example, the fact that a girl child has just the same opportunities as a boy. Of course girls have always been cleverer than boys, but the men haven't wanted to admit it, because they've got by on strength alone.

My wife certainly knew this. She sure would have liked a girl child.

My daughter-in-law had them.

Today a girl can go to school and then go abroad to study engineering or to the next parish to the crafts college to train as a fuller.

Could my wife hear my thoughts? Could my daughter-in-law? They should hear, so that they could learn and understand.

Girls, too, should remember the essentials. The first can still be the best. When you find the right man, you should let him open the door and carry the food shopping if he wants to. And from time to time you should cook him burgers with onions, even if he says he can do it himself. Or whatever soya burgers you like to have today.

My oldest grandchild is now eighteen, nearly grown up. But today eighteen summers is almost a child, at most a young person. And the whole world is wide open to her.

When I was a little boy, a child had the responsibilities of an adult. In poor homes children had jobs to do, otherwise we would not have got by. In those days an eighteen-year-old had been working for a long time and had started a family. If the same situation arose today, it would be the subject of newspaper articles and television interviews.

There is a lot of talk about equality, and there are a lot of theories, although actually it's a question of numbers. You get what you realise you should give. In exchange you may get soya soup, a new dress, a baby or a foreign holiday. I once planned something like that. All through the Seventies I planned a trip to Gotland, and even learned some Swedish. *Goodaa. Hoor more doo. Vee vil har kaffe tak.*

Does my wife remember?

Does my daughter-in-law?

Which of them was beside me – was either of them?

But if you have a boy in the family, you need to be careful. I would teach him to fish, to insulate and to mend. But those skills may well be the wrong ones, useless, because you have to be able to talk, to read and to type on computer networks. And then you have to master listening and caring.

The world sure is beginning to be so perfectly complete that menders and renovators are no longer needed. People are complete, perfect, in the same way. They're so healthy that cuppers or tooth-pullers are no longer necessary, only head-therapists.

It seems like a world for girls and women. Boys have to adapt to it.

I tried to focus my gaze, but the shapes remained dim.

I even took them in my arms a couple of times, the children. I lifted them up to the light to see if their cheeks were round. My son peed in my face in that position. I told him the farm would be his one day. I told him which corner to start the ploughing and whom to trust in a tight situation. And that Father's rifle, and a box of bullets, were hidden under some sawdust in the attic. When I heard my wife coming from the kitchen into the bedroom, I put my son back in his bed and promised to turn our smallholding into a farm.

That didn't happen. But life doesn't go as you hope, and your hopes, too, change. What you hoped for earlier can happen too late.

I felt a needle in my arm.

Was it Kivinkinen who was giving the injection, was it already the comfort syringe I'd asked for? Or was I in the Ski Club's ambulance, was Kyrö the trainer preparing me for the senior citizens' fifty-kilometre race?

Soon after their birth, children are already eight years old. The night terrors are a thing of the past, clearing up overturned glasses of milk is a thing of the past, little ones begin to be more of a help than a hindrance. The way people are made, they forget hard times once a hard time is over. Unless it's an absolutely impossible hard time, torture or overpopulation.

And seventy-six, and still they are someone's child, even though their parents lie in their graves.

After all, we're here because we're born as someone's brat. That someone watches us and feeds us and clothes us and gives us a cuff on the ear and hot chocolate and helps with our homework and shows us how to turn over and how to work with our hands and gives us some hints as to who we should be friends with and what kind of a life you can have if you start your career early. The brat becomes bigger than itself and makes more brats. The brats then have to carry us fathers and mothers to our graves or put them on a pyre or whatever it is they do, preserve us in formaldehyde for future scientists, in case they invent eternal life in addition to gelling agents.

At some point every child is difficult, but at the end of the evening everything is fine as they snuffle in their beds. Or, as adults, they have come round for the evening and you see the car's reversing lights and you can still wave to them for a moment from the outside steps even though you know they can no longer see you.

That's the kind of thing I talked about in my sleep, although I might have been awake, and then I slumped as if sinking into a haystack. Or taking a dip, on the hottest day in July, in a warm bend in the river.

I asked if my wife could hear me.

But it could be that I didn't ask; it could be that there was no one there.

*

Are there potatoes in heaven?

Well, it sure ruined my day when I woke up from my death to the sound of the morning radio. The loudspeaker was broadcasting drivel with an emphasis on youth music. I had to be either alive or in the deepest reaches of hell, because in heaven there are no morning radio programmes, just Arvi Lind reading the ordinary news.

The male radio presenter was talking about what had happened to him the previous day at the food shop and this made the female presenter laugh a lot. She responded by saying how difficult it was to find the right kind of shoes now that it had finally snowed.

Talking nonsense suddenly became a job. In times gone by the only people who were allowed to talk nonsense were politicians and Martti Hulkkonen in the

Pilsner bar next to the co-op. Then times changed and some folk were able to let go of their shovels. Their lips started moving and have never stopped.

I can understand the professions of newsreader and Moscow correspondent. That is proper talk, with pictures of what's being talked about, revolutions or SALT treaties. People should know about things that are bigger than themselves. War zones, earthquakes and Olympic medals. But radio waves and TV time should not be used to reveal private lives.

I tried to reach over to turn the radio off, but my hand didn't move.

Neither hand, and neither foot.

Perhaps I had died after all.

Perhaps there is no horned one or fiery furnace in hell, just a constant babble of Terhi or Mikkis-Lakkis and yeah-yeah-yeah music and advertisements for electrical shops.

I would have accepted that kind of death. Falling onto the floor out of one's own coffin would look good in the newspaper and the pathological report, as long as both of them remembered to describe the hinges and upholstery the dead man had made.

If I had died, I would surely not be lying in a soft bed. I glanced down at my chest to see whether I was still wearing the white shirt and suit that Kolehmainen's wife had given me. I wasn't. What I had on was a sand-brown pair of pyjamas and a blue blanket.

My eyes moved.

I glanced around me and saw big windows and the venetian blinds that covered them. Beyond them it was snowing. I began to feel like going on a ski trip, but I was a prisoner in my bed and forced to listen to a music talk that was beginning on the radio. Young people can't even be bothered to sing any more; instead they put a background beat on their machines and talk over it. Then they clap their hands and slap their bottoms as if they had a bad case of pinworm. The words are supposed to rhyme, but it sure would be worth those beanie-wearers going to the library to read the classic poet Eino Leino and listen to the folk singer and satirist Jaakko Teppo.

I was frightened: what if I was in heaven after all? How can anyone know what heaven is like? No one has ever come back to say, or to ask if they could have some rye bread and salt liquorice because there's none there, or a Mediterranean climate. I have my doubts as to whether Saint Peter is waiting for us at heaven's gate. And when you get a pass from him, then on the other side of the gate your relatives and friends are waiting for you.

What age would those relatives be? Are they as they were when they died? Do they use a walker to move along the clouds, or do they wear ice-fishing overalls, like Unto, who fell through the spring ice?

If a man has died in war, does he have to accept his wife Kaarina, who has lived to be ninety-eight? What if, as a widow, Kaarina has found another friend? What if the dead soldier finds a new and better spouse in heaven?

Who will he spend eternity with? Will the family quarrels and explanations begin – I found him in my loneliness and not just out of lust? Can you practise polygamy in heaven? Do the same rules hold there, or is there a freer interpretation? What if the flames of hell await one spouse, while the other gets into the kingdom of heaven? What kind of heaven is it if you have to be alone there?

This is how it is: people invented heaven as soon as they began to understand how the world works. As soon as they began to walk on two legs. They understood that they would die and were very afraid. They had to invent a back door. Even the Neanderthals thought that a brother who died in a fight with a mammoth would go to a good place and not languish in a Siberian salt mine. Or a mother or a father or particularly one's own little child. For thousands of years it has been easier to think that when everything is over you will be able to lie back and relax on a soft cloud, beside the good Father. For a person who has never been able to take naps or have cream pastries for pudding it is easy to believe the babble that says that heaven has everything you could wish for.

These sorts of groundless promises have always suited lords in their castles, provosts and pop stars. It is easy to promise little Pentti a better life sometime in the future, over there in a different province; but now, you landless and toothless wretch, you can till my land, tend my cattle and set the diamonds in my goblets. The landless went to church, feared nature and God, and believed that bliss would dawn one day. They endured famines, leprosy, earth-floored cabins and conscription while the earl ate a fatty roast, tickled young girls and slurped sweet wines.

Heaven, for earls and millionaires, has always been right here on earth. They have always known the truth, but have just neglected to share it with the people.

All over the world people have their own beliefs. The A-Studio radio programme says that according to Khomeini's people a row of virgins awaits a suicide-bomber. I have often wondered who on earth would want an unknown virgin for himself? What would you say to her? Where would you put your hands? Would she be in her birthday suit or wearing a dress? Are you expected to start romping with seventy-two virgins even though you blew yourself up into a thousand pieces just a moment ago? Are you allowed to decline the offer? Are the virgins decent working folk, presumably not.

In that debate, some language expert said that those virgins were raisins in the original text – that it was wrongly translated.

This information sure doesn't change the problem to any extent. What would a suicide-bomber do with raisins? Get a stomach-ache, and you can't eat raisin soup for ever, however much you liked it as a child.

It occurred to me that heaven could be like the kind of room I had found myself in. Snowfall beyond the venetian blinds, the radio prattling in my ears. My ability to move taken away, likewise my sense of direction. I sure would be sorry if my eternity were to be spent here.

My thoughts were moving at an impossible speed, even though my hands and feet did not move at all. Had I had a stroke, like Arvo Suurpenikka who, in 'Forty seven, fell off some scaffolding? The same bloke had survived three wars without a scratch and then happened to be sitting in the wrong place on his coffee break. I still remember what he was talking about. A smile on his face, he was telling us about a water diviner who had visited their garden, holding a twig in his hand, explaining how he knew where the best water source was. Halfway through a sentence he tipped over and fell head first to the ground. Even though he fell onto gravel, you could hear the crack as far back as where we were sitting. There were no emergency helicopters or ambulances in those days. A horse pulled Arvo to the Kylmäsuo crossroads and we had to wait three hours for the post bus. I tried to think of something to say to Arvo, but I couldn't think of anything except that you never knew, it might turn out for the best. A few weeks later I was supposed to go with the others to visit him in the hospital, but I couldn't do it. A man of working age there at the mercy of others, drool dripping from his lips, while I could still walk on two legs and use my hands.

I attempted to make a sound, but all that came out of my mouth was rattling and fizzing. I tried to turn my head, and succeeded in moving it a couple of centimetres. From the non-existent colour of the walls and the bedclothes I surmised I was in an institution. Not a prison, as there were no bars, and innocent people of my age are no longer put even in a black Maria. I wasn't in a school either, as there were no desks.

I noticed the movement of another living being, or more accurately the lack of movement. In the next bed lay a figure whose head was bound with bandages and plaster. One of its legs was also in plaster. The skin of the cheeks was fatty in a way that suggested a young man, as did the fact that next to him sat a woman, who looked more like a mother than a wife. You could see it in the expression, and also in the breathing. On the bedside cabinet was a pile of magazines, electronic devices and plates of food.

I tried to get words, or even sounds, out of my mouth.

My palate was absolutely dry and my tongue motionless as it had been during the only hangover of my life. I have no idea why a person has to wake up without any memory of a Kymenlaakso sauna from which it had taken three days to get home. I hadn't been able to thumb a lift and my wallet was missing. Later I calculated from the map that I had walked 250 kilometres. After that I decided that from now on, a mug of booze would suffice. Any more meant sick days and organ transplants, which is a high price to pay for the couple of hours of cheerfulness at the beginning of a bender.

The mummy's mother noticed my gagging and turned toward me. She took a glass from the bedside cabinet and helped me take a gulp. I sure was grateful, and really angry, at the same time. I hadn't been helped to drink since I was a child, and not very often even then, because as soon as I could stand on my own two feet I was carrying two full buckets of water inside.

I could whisper a little and asked for Finland.

'I'm sorry? We're in Finland. We do speak Finnish.'

Radio Finland. Now.

The woman looked around her and shrugged her shoulders as if she did not understand, or else she thought me wrong in the head. I said I was the oldest person in the room and the oldest person decides on the channel, even though I did not know where I was. Morning cheerfulness over, then the news, weather and sport. Although even there, these days, all they do is list the temperature in cities I will never go to.

'They always have this channel on here,' the woman said, clearly not understanding the gravity of the situation.

The Week in Politics and *Nature Evening* could still save the day after my death. And what will happen if the woman's son has to stay in hospital for a long spell and all that is being fed into his ears are sponsored programmes. The mummy will become the same kind of propaganda victim as the Soviets and members of the German youth in the Thirties.

The woman got up from her chair and looked round for the radio. I moved my head as much as possible, but I could not see a radio receiver anywhere. But I could see a third patient in the bed next to the corridor.

He was yellow and was making a sucking movement with his lips as if a big gob of spit were coming. His bed had been raised into a sitting position. He was reading an inappropriate magazine.

I sure did wonder where the man had got his copy of *Smile* magazine, because hospital wards don't have *Smile*, only *Finland's Picture Magazine, The Future of the Countryside* and *Country News. Smile* magazine shows titties and tells stories that appeal to people's baser instincts. I've leafed through it at the barber's. There was a story about a man who got up to some mischief with animals and was dragged through Lieksa by a tractor.

I sure did wonder then, and wonder now, why people are so fascinated by these nasty stories. Do we have to know everything? Is it necessary to reveal that a politician has a mistress, if he's performing successfully in one-to-one negotiations and trade agreements? Is Africa really nothing but misery, hunger, viruses and demented tyrants? Doesn't anything good ever happen there? Are the streets of Russia eternally full of slush and weeping grannies, as the news would have you believe?

People sure should write about ordinary things.

I have drafted a letter on the subject to the three biggest media companies, but of course no one answers, because there is no one there anymore. The lead story in the first issue would have been Kaisa Mahonen's November Tuesday morning, when she thought that she had run out of coffee but found a new packet in the cupboard. Her husband would have said that for his wife even bad coffee is best. They would have been photographed together, coffee cups in hand. The packet would not have been shown, because it is unnecessary to say out loud that Juhla Mokka is the best brand, and on Sundays Presidentti.

On the magazine's technology pages I could have learnt how to get the petrol consumption of the Escort below six litres. The sports pages would have carried a story about Ilmari Tilkkinen's nephew's perfectly waxed skis in the third part of the cross-country ski competition. It wasn't nearly enough, of course, because Tilkkinen was in poor shape and lazy. But that doesn't take away the success of the waxing.

'I always keep *Smile* in my coat pocket,' said the man. I had evidently spoken my opinions aloud. 'I have a reason for it, too, if only I could remember it. Perhaps it's that when no one else is smiling at least the magazine is.'

I sure didn't consider that a plausible argument.

The man said he spent so much time in the institution that he always knew what he wanted to read while he was waiting. His hip hadn't improved after the fracture and neither had his weakness for alcohol. It is difficult to stay upright when one of your legs won't carry your weight.

I asked the man where he came from, since he didn't look at all familiar.

'I was born in Töölö. Brought up in Sörnäinen. We were in Malmi with the family as long as there was a family. After that here and there. More there.'

They sure were unfamiliar places to me. I asked the man his name.

'Pasanen.'

Old Man Pasanen?

'Nah.'

Viljami Pasanen?

'Nah.'

Old Man or Viljami's son Harri Pasanen? Santeri Pasanen?

'Isto Pasanen's middle boy. Just call me Sepi.'

It sure is Pertti who comes first to mind of all the Pasanens. Followed by my opinions of Pertti Pasanen's films: not good. One joke really can't carry an entire movie. Film-makers should think seriously why they are filming a made-up story, and this is also true of writers' books and theatre folk's plays. Worst of all are the sequels that are written out of laziness and a desire for money. In Pertti Pasanen's numbers a gap-toothed man lies on a sofa or falls over in the street. He doesn't want to do anything but eat frankfurters and chat with Sörssellssön.

Vesa-Matti Loiri was a good football goalie and handball goalie and that was what he should have concentrated on. But he just *had* to be a bad flute-player and a peculiar actor. On the other hand it would be worth this hospital-Pasanen fellow's while to follow Vesa-Matti's example of how to fall without hurting your head.

'Time to eat soon,' Pasanen said.

I remembered another Pasanen.

'I should probably go for a smoke.'

Tauno.

The director Mikko Niskanen made a film about him that lasted three days, in which Vesa-Matti Loiri, fortunately, didn't appear. Or actually, he should have appeared because falling over might have livened up the story. *Eight Fatal Bullets* basically describes the life of a smallholder very adequately. Gradually everything goes hopelessly wrong. An adult sure should know that there will be problems with the police chief if you distil liquor with the bloke next door. Of course you are going to run out of money if you lie around with your beer buddies in front of the farmhouse stove.

The law is the law. Fines are fines. Mistakes are made, and then you carry on. I could have said that to Pasanen.

I went to earn Finnish marks in the building trade when my own smallholding didn't produce enough. It was a pity, but what kind of solution would booze have been? When building work tailed off, I wondered for a while whether I should follow the others to Sweden. Perhaps I would have done, if they'd made Ford Escorts in Gothenburg instead of Volvos.

I said I was prepared to put up with Pasanen and the mummy. Pasanen declared that he wasn't necessarily in need of my tolerance.

I said what my daughter-in-law would have said: we all need each other's tolerance. When the conversation with Pasanen dried up, I asked the mummy's mother how I could get downstairs. Pasanen asked me to go with him: he could offer me a cigarette if I would buy him a coffee. I said I didn't smoke; I only wanted to go downstairs because my wife needed feeding. According to the mummy's mother all there was downstairs was a cellar and staff area. I corrected her, saying that the newly restored Kuusikoti Wing was certainly to be found down there.

'Where do you think you are?'

In the health centre ward.

'We're in Meilahti.'

I know Köykänlahti and Katuvalahti, but there is no Meilahti near us. Which town was I in, and why?

'This is the Helsinki University Central Hospital.'

Why have I been brought here? How can I get out of here?

'Errm, this is . . . this is the neurology department and you have been here since yesterday because . . .'

Neuro what?

'Head injuries.'

I sure did have to stop for a moment to think about what I had just heard. I asked whether I looked as if I had brain damage. Because I could no longer feel my hands or my feet. The woman moved back to her son. She fed him juice through a straw and said in a low voice that her son had been cycling home from a party when he fell. Pasanen said he had fallen countless times without a helmet during the last war, but something had always saved him from the worst. A rubbish bin, a bank of snow, the decking of a restaurant terrace, a friend. The mummy-boy's mother didn't say anything. Pasanen twisted himself round and got out of bed by himself, just leaning on the wall a little for support.

Glancing upward, I tried to see whether I had some kind of plaster cast or net. I asked the mummy's mother. She said there was a fine gauze on the back of my head, nothing else. I tried to shake my body as you always do when you wake up in a cold room to get all the muscles in the body to engage. Nothing happened. I asked the mummy's mother to pinch me.

'Please don't.'

Could you pinch me really hard on the neck, for example? Don't you think an old person has the right to know whether he can still feel anything?

The mummy's mother thought for a second and then turned towards me. She looked me in the eyes and asked me if I was serious. I promised to swear with my hand on a Ford Escort repair manual, if my hand were ever to move again. The woman put her fingers and her nails on my neck and pinched. At first I wasn't sure whether I could feel anything, because I am so used to not showing pain. I asked her to pinch harder. This time I bellowed so loudly that a nurse rushed into the room, followed by a doctor. They wondered what had happened and moved the mummy's mother away from me.

I said I had received help in my lack of sensation from the neighbouring bed, although not from the staff, so there was no problem here.

The doctor took my file from the nurse, disregarded my words and leafed through the papers. He took my hand in his and felt my pulse. He said something to the nurse, who wrote down the information. Then a strange sort of thermometer was pushed into my ear; it was apparently able to take my temperature in seconds. According to the doctor there was too much wax in there, a piece of information which in my opinion it was not necessary to share with the other people in the room.

Something about the pinching had been successful, because gradually heat and sensation began to return to my body. I still could not move my hands or my feet, but I knew they were there. I asked what was wrong with me.

'Concussion.'

Please speak Finnish.

'Shock,' said the mummy's mother from the next bed.

I thanked the boy. I asked his name, but according to the doctor we had to concentrate on one patient at a time. But the doctor agreed with the boy's version of what was wrong with me. I asked why Kivinkinen wasn't looking after me.

'Are you confusing me with someone else? Can you tell me what day it is today? Who is the president?'

I suggested I list the presidents of Finland in alphabetical order along with the years of their wives' birth. The doctor could then tell me, for example, their years in office.

When we had argued for a while, I demanded to see Dr Kivinkinen again.

'There is no one of that name here, my dear sir. You are now in an intensive care unit.'

I sure want to be in a normal care unit.

We went on talking like this for a while without making contact with each other. Because of my dozing and delirium, the city doctor wanted to keep me on as an inpatient. He insisted on the necessity of taking magnetic images and carrying out all sorts of tests as if I were some Olympic athlete. After that there would be rehabilitation. I asked when I would go home.

I asked who was looking after my wife while I was not there. The doctor did not know who I was talking about and again he told the nurse to write something down. They clearly considered me a nutcase and not a man who had yesterday finished making his own coffin.

Pasanen came back from his cigarette break and got into his bed. The doctor and nurse moved on to him. Pasanen was given a new bandage, fed his medications under observation and then given some kind of injection. The mummy's bed, on the other hand, was pushed out of the room entirely; he was being taken somewhere for a scan.

Pasanen fell asleep quickly and began to snore. It was a homely sound, reminding me of when, as a young man at the lumber camp, there could be as many as ten of us lying on a big bunk, each of us snoring louder than the next. But our work, and our bread, were so hard that sleep came without any problems.

When all the sounds had disappeared, I noticed that the radio channel was still the same one. I took a paper towel from the bedside cabinet, moistened it with spit, made balls and pushed them into my ears.

Grandpa's porpoise

I don't know what the time was or who was speaking somewhere near me. I didn't open my eyes because I wanted get my thoughts in line with the time and place. My earplugs had fallen out and I could hear speech clearly from close by. The voices were those of my daughter-in-law and my son and they clearly thought I was asleep.

'We're supposed to fill in this form,' my son said. 'I suppose it would be easiest if we filled it in . . . together.'

My daughter-in-law took the piece of paper and all was quiet for a moment.

'Have you got a pen?'

My son must have nodded in agreement, because my daughter-in-law read from the form:

'One: describe the important relationships within your family and amongst your friends which it will be necessary to uphold during your treatment.'

It sure was the familiar old stuff. It was called a life-cycle form and it included many difficult questions. Dr Kivinkinen had asked me to fill one out for my wife. At that point he explained that in the health centre ward they needed to know where a person came from, with what kind of thoughts and hopes. Particularly since my wife and people like her didn't say an awful lot about themselves after they arrived on the ward. The answers were supposed to help the staff who would work with my wife every day.

I had my doubts about answering personal questions on another person's behalf. Most of all I wondered why my son and my daughter-in-law were now filling in a similar form for me.

'Dad doesn't have any friends,' my son said to my daughter-in-law. 'Although he knows everyone. Yrjänä is dead.'

'Am I supposed to write that on the form? Maybe, I don't know and that Yrjänä is dead.'

'Don't blame me,' my son answered. 'Put my name and phone number. We're his closest relatives, you, me and the children. Aren't we?'

One best friend is enough in a life. You can also have a couple of fishing buddies and someone to agree with that this year, once again, the ten thousand metres won't be run in less than twenty-eight minutes. To talk about the weather and the depth of snow compared to last year.

There was a moment's silence as my daughter-in-law wrote the answer on the form and read the next question.

'Important social roles. In brackets, for example, grandfather or grandmother.'

When I was filling in the form for my wife I wondered what kind of social role that really was. Socialist roles I know, Karl Marx, Mr Lenin and Karri Paasonen – a really good man with concrete, but he went on about the dictatorship of the proletariat and the common ownership of the means of production. My wife and I didn't have any roles, since we're real people and not actors.

'Dad's not really a traditional grandfather . . .' my son pondered.

'Isn't he?' my daughter-in-law answered quickly. 'Not traditional? Is he innovative? Modern? I'd say he was a patriarch.'

I heard a third chair being drawn up beside my son and my daughter-in-law. The person who sat down was light, as the chair didn't bump or scratch the floor.

'He's Grandpa,' a voice said.

It was my oldest granddaughter, and now the situation became interesting. I felt like saying it was useless to think too much about the answers to the questions, because the first answers to come to mind were right.

'Mum, give me the form.'

'Hey, what are you doing . . .'

'I'm writing on the form since you're just messing around. G, R, A, N, D, P, A.'

My granddaughter wrote more on the form before moving on to the next question.

'Most important personality traits and temperament?'

Another chair was drawn up beside the bed.

'What does temperamentary mean?' asked my smaller grandchild.

'Almost the same as personality,' said my daughter-in-law. 'Or maybe more. You sure can see the temperament of a person quickly. Like in all of you. One is considerate. Another explodes if there is more than three hours between meals. The third isn't afraid of anything and is always in need of a plaster.'

'But what's Grandpa's pentera . . . mentera . . . temparamint?'

'Pig-headed,' my son suggested

'Know-all,' my daughter-in-law said.

'What's a know-all?'

'Mum, you're much more pig-headed than he is,' my older granddaughter said. 'I'm not going to put that he's a pig-headed know-all.'

'I think he was . . . he is steady,' my son said. 'Sort of resistant to change. Maybe in a kind of way stifling too . . .'

I wrote on my wife's form that she was a good worker and that the children were always fed and clothed. Always made me my coffee, never had a bad word against anyone.

'They don't get any easier,' said my granddaughter. 'World view and values?'

They were such big words that on my wife's form I made them smaller. I said she was an ordinary person for whom the ordinary was enough.

'A hippy,' my daughter-in-law suggested.

Then they laughed, and it wasn't unkind laughter, you sure can tell the difference. They imagined me with long hair, hemp clothes and ridiculously free opinions.

'One of the lads,' said my son.

That only amused my son and my daughter-in-law.

'Take it easy,' my granddaughter begged. 'Isn't Grandpa kind of conservative and radical at the same time?'

Of my wife's world view and values I stated that she looks at everything with open eyes. Home and family are important and she intends to hold to her faith because she believes she knows God and Jesus personally.

'Let's not use big words, because Grandpa himself wouldn't use them. I'll call him an upholder.'

Good girl, clever girl. Just like her grandma.

'Things that might give pleasure and delight?'

For my wife, it was the changing of the seasons and a flock of cranes.

'Everyone likes their nearest and dearest to visit,' my daughter-in-law pondered. 'So that they know they aren't alone.'

Silence, the rustle of paper. Legs were crossed and uncrossed and the chairs creaked a little. Pasanen coughed and hawked in his bed.

'I don't really . . .' my son sighed. 'I see it now . . . I don't really know anything about my father.'

Do you need to know about anyone? Isn't it enough to know about yourself and to remember how tall you are, what food you like and whether it's time to go to bed. So much importance is placed on talking in today's world, even though it's lighter than air. I heard the scratch of pen on paper. My granddaughter went on with the form:

'Things that cause pain and anxiety?'

My son was silent, but it was his response the others were waiting for.

'Once I asked whether Dad was afraid during the war,' he said.

'What did Grandpa say?'

'Should I go and look at the fish trap.'

You don't want to pass your own burdens on to your children, particularly when you know they cannot understand them. I saw on the television how at one time the bearded radicals turned everything upside down, making attackers into defenders and sensible people into extremists.

'So he *was* afraid,' my oldest grandchild said. 'If he hadn't been afraid, he would have said no straight away.'

My granddaughter was clearly the most intelligent person in the room. She said the next question was even more difficult than the last. It wanted to know about my attitudes to myself, to other people and to death.

'I'd say he's a fatalist,' my son said immediately.

'What's a fatanist?' asked my smaller granddaughter.

'It means you take things as they come. You understand that everything has its purpose.'

'What's a porpoise? Why doesn't everyone have a porpoise? Does Grandpa have a porpoise?'

On my wife's form I wrote that she has a helpful attitude towards other people. But I didn't understand the question about her attitude to herself. How can you have an attitude to yourself, when you're you? About her attitude to death, I knew what my wife often said. The Lord giveth and the Lord taketh away.

'Dad isn't afraid of death,' my son said.

'Everyone's afraid,' my daughter-in-law answered. 'Even if they don't admit it they're afraid.'

'How can you know?' my son asked.

'And what about this one: his attitude to himself and to others?' my granddaughter asked.

'High expectations,' my son said. 'That's what you'd say if Dad was an ice-hockey coach. Or a film director.'

'Did he teach you religious habits?' my granddaughter asked. 'Like, as a child. Did you pray at night?'

I sure would have taught my children all sorts of things, if they had been prepared to learn. I took them skiing and into the forest. I took them with me to slaughter pigs, but they ran away in tears. They didn't like to be on the lake, dreaming of fish fingers from the freezer.

'He taught me that it's not worth doing things badly if you can do them well,' my son said, and the sentence ended, somehow tailing off.

'When will Grandpa wake up?' the little one asked. 'Will it be long? Can we go for an ice-cweam when Grandpa wakes up? Wake up, Grandpa!'

I heard my son getting up out of his chair and going somewhere nearby. Perhaps he was looking out of the window.

The next question asked about the patient's hobbies and favourite activities. On my wife's form I wrote making coffee, going to the sauna and, in the winter, cross-country skiing. And talking to her sister on the telephone.

'Dad doesn't have hobbies,' my son pondered. 'He did everything for real. Does. Did.'

Then my son said something that should have remained a secret between the two of us:

'He liked knitting . . .'

'What are you talking about,' my granddaughter said.

'Yes, yes. He said so in his obituary.'

'What obituary?'

'In the Escort. Or . . . it's a long story. Knitting, anyway . . .'

Enough of this. This was another thing I should do myself.

They froze when I opened my eyes and said that my hobbies were cross-country skiing and woodwork.

My younger granddaughter smiled broadly; one of her grown-up teeth was already in place. She climbed on to the foot of the bed and began to introduce me to her doll, which had a foreign name. I shook hands with the doll and asked if it was time for coffee.

'You heard everything just now?' my son asked, and I had only to look him in the eye for him to understand my answer. He went red all over as if he had just run a long way in a second.

'Now there's a question about his own family,' my granddaughter read.

A green cardboard box in my workshop cupboard. In it are photographs taken over the course of a hundred years. They are archived and on the back of each is written who everyone is, study them. There are many families, of which each has led to your family.

After I had spoken I glanced at my daughter-in-law, who crossed her hands over her chest and looked back.

I told my son to look in particular at a picture with Reino Iso-Mattila in it. Our family features are at their strongest in him; he looks equally like all of us. He was a tanner by trade. If you don't know what that is, you can look it up on your global computer networks.

I encouraged my daughter-in-law to look at the photographs of mothers with their babies, and fathers too, in the newer pictures.

And bigger siblings. It looks more like a good and sufficient life than terrible misery.

When the life-cycle form was ready, I wanted to buy coffee and cardamom *pulla* buns for everyone, or alternatively ice creams, but my wallet was in the pocket of my trousers at home. I asked my daughter-in-law for a pen and took a napkin from the bedside cabinet. I wrote a list of jobs for my son.

From home I needed my wallet, a clean pair of trousers, a fountain pen and some white paper. My wife was to be fed, and the snow cleared, if more snow came. He should check the coffee machine was turned off and the attic window closed.

I advised they should boil the potatoes in advance at home until they were soft. Then just mash them with a fork and mix them with butter and no need to skimp. Then my wife also likes it when you put a grain of salt right there under her tongue and when it has melted, then exchange it for a piece of sugar.

My son wondered if he really had to leave straight away, but I didn't even bother to answer. He looked at my daughter-in-law, seeking a yes or no. When he didn't get one, he told the children he would be back in a couple of days. I supposed he was embarrassed about what he'd said when he thought I was asleep.

My daughter-in-law and my grandchildren stayed for a moment longer and I listened to my grandchildren's stories about school, the origins of the world and climate change.

Only after they had gone did I understand what had happened. I had written a list for my son and my hand hadn't trembled at all.

Delighted, I tried to get to my feet and noticed a small problem.

My hands worked; my feet didn't.

My health, my youth

Even just to stand I needed the wall for support, or Pasanen, who couldn't stand upright any better than I could. When I tried to move it felt as if I were a one-year-old crawler, or a slacker who had boozed all his life.

I asked Pasanen, on one of his cigarette breaks, to bring back a bar of chocolate from the café because I suspected there were deficiencies in my blood sugar. I have never eaten chocolate rolls before; frozen lingonberries have always been enough to satisfy my cravings for sweet things, and peas in summertime. Turnips are sweet when boiled. Chocolate was no use, it just gave me a searing pain in my molars.

I drank a jugful of water, in case I was dehydrated. Then I needed to go to the loo urgently. I couldn't get there under my own steam but luckily the nurse guessed the nature of my emergency. She sat me down forcefully in a wheelchair and pushed me to the loo. She asked me if I could manage on my own from the door onwards. I used all my will and all that remained of my energy for the job.

The following day I asked the doctor to bring me the vitamin pills that Yrjänä took at the end, but their effect was clear thoughts and even wobblier legs than before.

They wanted to move me to make way for new patients. The hospital conveyor belt had a clear order, like in a factory. First the most intensive care, then stabilising care and finally rehabilitation.

'We have a good care plan,' the doctor explained. 'Soon you will be able to continue your life as before.'

I asked the doctor to specify which time of my life he meant. 'Fifty-four, when everything was still fine? Could we go to the year when the sprinter Voitto Hellsten closed the impossible Swedish lead in the last part of the Finland-Sweden Athletics International? Or did they mean the year 'O-nine or 'Ten, to which there's no point in returning.

Many fields I have tilled, many fish traps have I lifted, many Olympics have I seen, many foundations have I cast; I have pushed my children forward, grown grain, mended, patched and birthed calves and carried men of the family and of the village to the grave, but nevertheless there is nothing I can do about the fact that in the end a man sits in a wheelchair pushed by his daughter-in-law.

I grabbed control of the wheels myself. I pushed for speed; the wheelchair went like the Escort on a newly laid Tarmac road. My smallest grandchild jumped into my lap and demanded to go faster, faster. I accelerated simply because my hand worked and obeyed me. My daughter-in-law ran after us in her clattery shoes and told me to watch out for walls, tables and oncoming patients. I reminded her that I had driven the Escort for forty years without mishap. I would certainly be able to drive one wheelchair out of the hospital. I rolled into the open lift and let the child press the green button, the one that said 'G'.

Children like pressing buttons. They think they control this world, when in fact they control the movement of the lift or get a label for a bag of fruit from a weighing machine. I sure hope my granddaughter will sustain her hopefulness in later life.

On the entrance floor I continued, my grandchild in my lap, toward the door. In the vestibule people were shaking snowflakes from their coats. On the other side of the sliding doors I could see tall hospital buildings in all directions and I could also see Pasanen smoking one cigarette after another; beside him was an intravenous drip on wheels. They looked just like brothers or buddies, both of them as thin as rakes.

I left my thoughts unsaid: it will be expensive for society, in other words me, to pay for a liver transplant, or damage to property. A person of his age and experience should understand his own interests, because they are always the same as society's.

'Listen, old man,' Pasanan called out. 'If you come here again, bring the latest *Smile* magazine with you. Come on the fifteenth and I'll have my benefits in my account.'

My guess was that both our journeys were nearing their last stop, so there wouldn't be much time for surprise visits.

'That depends on how you look at it,' Pasanen said. 'Let's live a day at a time. We'll see, even if we stumble.'

My daughter-in-law panted up to us, complaining that we mustn't escape like that. I promised to escape considerably further and more convincingly as soon as I was able to. We looked at one another for a moment; there was some kind of battle of wills in progress. With the children you sometimes got locked like this for seconds on end until you thought of something that would stop the whingeing. When I was very tired I'd sometimes bellow so loudly that my younger son's eyes filled with tears. After that, my wife and if I would lock gazes if I was in a really bad mood, and tears would fill her eyes as well. It sure isn't easy to say you're sorry.

My granddaughter asked why I was wearing the president's suit, when generally Grandpa wore Grandpa's suit. I said I was practising for an important celebration. My granddaughter asked if any princesses would be coming to the party.

'I have a pwincess dress, a wimming costume, and dungawees,' she said.

They all sure are princess clothes, if that's what you want them to be.

The ambulance drove up the ramp and I was lifted in, sitting in the wheelchair. My daughter-in-law asked if I had everything with me; did I need anything from the ward or from the café.

I could have my health and my youth back for a moment.

I asked whether we were going to the physiotherapist; this would be the only good point about this accident, because the rehabilitation centre is located in the building next to my wife's ward. The ambulance man estimated our destination as about three kilometres away.

'There are better resources in Helsinki than at home,' my daughter-in-law said. 'They have the equipment and the staff.'

I sat with my back to the engine and didn't say anything else. Why should I be rehabilitated? My fitness comes from the Thirties, the bog, the forest, the Finnish baseball pitch, the forest path, ski trips and post-war reconstruction. This original machinery can't be helped by today's gadgets and manuals.

I sure didn't feel like doing anything any more, least of all thinking about myself. So I shifted the conversation to my daughter-in-law and my son. I asked what they intended to do about their problem, or in other words, their opportunity.

'What are you talking about?' my daughter-in-law asked as if she didn't know exactly what I meant.

The grub.

'What grub?' my oldest granddaughter asked.

'Grubs are great,' the middle one said.

My daughter-in-law raised a finger to her lips. It was directed both at me and at the children.

'We've already talked about it.'

When was that?

'On the last ambulance trip.'

We stopped at some traffic lights; the tram next to us got off to a quicker start.

My daughter-in-law noticed my uncertainty and said she had found me in my workshop with a bloody head. I asked whether it was she who had knocked on the door. My daughter-in-law nodded.

'I was afraid you were dead.'

I asked if I had been completely unconscious, like Harri Siippainen when the pine stump bounced on his forehead during felling.

'It's hard to compare you to Harri Siippainen here.'

It's not hard. He was a short man; I'm short-to-medium.

'Hessu and I had just been talking about the will you were writing,' my daughter-in-law said. 'About the coffin. About all this. We were afraid you might do something to yourself.'

I really am not a suicide man. I will take the life of a fish, and I don't mind putting an end to rodents, but that's where the killing stops, for me. I have gone hunting with the boys, but I left the elk in peace. If someone were to threaten my life or my wife's or the children's, that's why there's a hunting rifle in sawdust in the attic. I'd aim for the foot or painfully at the side of the belly, but not at the internal organs.

Over the centuries in Finland we've invented an unbeatable way of surviving difficult situations. Namely, not talking.

'You sure talked then. Lots of words came out of your mouth. Chernobyl. Ski wax. Eero Mäntyranta. Rice pudding.'

I considered those perfectly adequate as last words, but I didn't like it that I didn't remember anything about the situation. When you're not your own master you may become someone's fool. My daughter-in-law said that the ambulance took us first to the central hospital of Middle Finland, but that we were then sent on to the capital.

I asked if I had any reason to be embarrassed, had I talked nonsense, did I make myself into a difficult case.

'It wasn't nonsense. You were talking complete sense. But now you're recovering, so let's concentrate on that. Hessu and I will look after you ourselves. You can take it easy and follow what they tell you to do here.'

At this age you have to take it easy if you want to take even one more step forward. The same stairs which you could leap at a bound in your youth now require six minutes. That's one of the reasons why it's worth having a lot of children, so they can help you.

I warned my daughter-in-law that she would be able to enjoy old age for considerably longer than I would. She was fed minerals and vegetables in the school canteen; her teeth are filled with fluoride. Osteoporosis is a long way off for my daughter-in-law. Her blood pressure is at a good level and she has money in the bank for private doctors when the public health service runs out of money.

My daughter-in-law nodded but said nothing.

The ambulance arrived outside a new hospital. My wheelchair was lowered to the ground by a lift-like contraption. Outside you can smell spring, autumn and winter dog poo, the strong pollen of flowers or a cigarette butt, but inside there's always the same institutional smell. It is a combination of all human smells and cleaning materials. I told my daughter-in-law that we sure aren't institutional people, but outdoor people.

'What on earth are you talking about?' my granddaughter asked. 'What do you mean? Is there something I should know about?'

Little, ordinary things, I said.

'Life and death,' my daughter-in-law said.

My smaller granddaughter stepped in through the sliding doors and said that children don't die but adults and elephants die, and Hilkka's granny. At funerals you throw sand on the coffin, at funerals it rains, at funerals you have to drink root beer.

News deficit

New hospital clothes again. Followed by the question, can I get changed by myself. I suggested to the nurse girl that I would be happy to exchange them for my work clothes. Or potatoes. The nurse could have smiled at my comments, but her workload and the shortage of beds made it necessary to forget laughter.

I was in room number three and this time my room-mate was a girl on an exercise bike.

'Normally our equipment room is separate,' the nurse explained. 'But there's water damage, so some of the machines have been moved on to the ward.'

I said I had my doubts about the hysteria a little spot of mould can cause these days. The best solution would be to get out of a rotting home and work in the garden. Offices and schools should be located outdoors; reports would be written more efficiently in twenty-three degrees of frost. Now there are all sorts of inspections and construction engineers are paid for things that you can clearly see with your own eyes. Those element-built ratholes of the Seventies shouldn't be inspected, but avoided. And replaced by something better, in wood.

When I greet the girl she has a boy's voice. Because she's a long-haired boy. Just when I've grown accustomed to the mummy and Pasanen I have to get to know a new person, even though I've always tried to avoid passing acquaintances.

I gave my view of long-haired boys: that they tune guitars and refuse to carry weapons. I said I approved of refusing to carry weapons if it's a question of conscience, and demands more guts than military service. If you refuse to bear arms just because your dad did and your brother did and your best friend did, then I urge you to reconsider. The same goes for military service. You shouldn't volunteer for the barracks on account of your grannies and granddads, or on account of war movies, but for yourself.

The boy thanked me for the information, but our conversation dried up there and then.

In the days that followed I was encouraged to use a series of mechanical and electric gadgets to help me stretch. I refused the treatment because I knew best what would help all my bodily ailments. Walking on my back. I asked the doctor, on his morning round, whether I could get a grant from social insurance to pay my six-year-old granddaughter. Her heels were just the right size to fit between my shoulder blades.

'We do not recommend self-care methods here,' the doctor answered. 'We follow a specific rehabilitation programme and you are welcome to acquaint yourself with it. On no account may external force or pressure be applied to your back.'

That is exactly what should be applied to it.

'What is happening here is, in plain language, a disturbance in the flow of information between your brain and your legs. Tomorrow we will take a magnetic image, then conduct some neurological examinations . . .'

Disturbance in the flow of information is right, but it's between the doctor's brain and my reality.

'Well, I suppose it is a good thing that your sense of humour is intact.'

The doctor had decided what was wrong and her orders were put into action. In the mornings the same memory tests in which I was asked who I was and where, what is six times six, and can I tell my right from my left.

To lie in a hospital bed doing nothing is different from doing nothing at home. The nights I spent in the rehabilitation hospital were the longest in my life.

There was one good day. My daughter-in-law brought me my own clothes, which my son had sent in the mail. He had taken my request seriously and was working hard at home. Going to feed his mother every day, and he intended to inspect the gutters, too.

In my trouser pocket I found my wallet and was able to pay my canteen debts and give my granddaughter money for ice cream.

The only activity in my lonely days was the eating of tasteless meals and arguing with the cyclist. Whenever I turned the television on, the cyclist switched it off.

'I don't believe in it,' the cyclist explained.

What?

'Television.'

The news sure isn't television or a matter of belief, but news. What does the cyclist believe in, then?

'The world soul.'

Of course.

'All religions come basically from the same source.'

Of course they do, they're all based on the same stories. That's exactly why we should watch the news bulletins, so we know what is true and what is fiction. If all you look at is violent videos, confectionery adverts and light music, what can you know of the world?

'It's easier if you don't know everything. There's such a ridiculous amount of knowledge that we're drowning in it.'

A person sure should know the basic facts. I asked him who held the Finnish 5,000 metres record and where it was run. And who came fourth in the race.

I turned the TV on.

The cyclist pulled the plug from the wall. He was beginning to be almost frightening. When I raised the subject with the nurse, she urged us to find a peaceful solution to the matter.

In the evening my first hours of sleep went awry because I was thinking about how to watch the news. I woke up at 4:27 and knew what to do. I summoned the night nurse and announced that I needed a telephone.

The very next day the civilised youth drew his chair up beside me and asked worriedly what had happened to me. I gave him an edited version of falling out of the coffin and of western medicine, which does not believe in the healing power of the heel in treating paralysis. In the youth's opinion it was worth trying anything if one thought it might help. Then the civilised youth got a lap television out of his bag.

'It's last year's model.'

Thank you. I will return it when I get out of here. The civilised youth said he was giving it to me for my very own because he got a new one as a school-leaving present. Last year's model was automatically old for him, but I might like it.

In my youth Pentti Lukkoinen got a set of false teeth for his school-leaving present. In my youth things got a new model once in a generation.

Tractors and radios lasted a human lifetime, but today a new version of a device is released at the very same moment as you learn to use the old one. The civilised youth smiled briefly and said he was extremely

fond of my extreme opinions. He said he had installed
all the programs I would need on the lap television.

Does that mean *Current Events* from 'Seventy-nine
on Channel Two? Or Paavo Noponen's coverage of the
Geneva winter sports? Or what about that film taken
from a helicopter on *Homeland Horizons*, where you
get a glimpse of our home village.

'Hang on a sec. You can find the news under this
icon. But first of all let's get a connection . . .'

The civilised youth tapped something into the lap
television and then put it in my hands. I was more
astonished than I can say when my wife's face appeared
on the screen.

I tried to maintain my serious expression, because
nothing surprises you much at this age. I asked the
civilised youth when he had visited Kuusikoti; the
young people of the capital only find their way there
if they're lost. And did the civilised youth have a
video camera with which he had recorded everything.
Then my son's face come on to the screen, smiling
slightly.

'Hi, Dad. You can already walk. Are you getting
treatment . . . Or are you in pain . . .?'

I looked at the civilised youth to ask what I should
talk into.

'Hello . . . are you there. I can see your face. Are you
there?'

I'm not there, but here. How on earth did the
civilised youth know that my wife was at Kuusikoti?

'It was easy,' he said. 'I found your opinion pieces on the local paper's website. So delightful.'

I did them under a pseudonym.

'I recognised your style immediately. You write in the same rhythm as you talk.'

I asked my son through the lap television whether he had given my wife something to eat. A picture of a plate appeared on the screen, with cut-up potatoes and then a fork mashing them. I asked whether my will papers and pen were safe. My son showed these, too, to the camera. I asked him to put them in the post, but my son said he was coming to town tomorrow. I would get everything I needed then.

'But hey, I need to get on with dinner. You know how mum can lose interest in eating really suddenly. Night night!'

I sure didn't understand in the least how I could be in contact with my wife, hundreds of kilometres away. In the old days I would have had to write to Hannu Karpo and ask him to make a report for next year's programme. And I wouldn't have been the only one to approach Hannu by letter or postcard, so I might have been at the back of the queue.

I've lived through a time when information moved at exactly the same speed as people. There were no cars in our village until the Forties and no telephone until Kalevi Ruuttainen and his wife Vilma got one in 1966. Many were the evenings when we went to look at it, but it never rang, because no one had anything to say to Ruuttainen. Four years later the slaughterman's house got a telephone and they began to call each other. We got our telephone when my wife absolutely demanded it.

'Wow, that's amazing,' the civilised youth said.

A smoke signal is a good invention and I would like them to become more popular, but they demand hills. How can you get a smoke signal into the air when there are forests everywhere? People wouldn't know if an important piece of information was arriving or if a serious forest fire had begun.

You had to wait a long time for bad news from the battlefront – many houses were in ignorance when letters and dead bodies began to be sent to the wrong villages and families. There was no certainty about election results until the time of the radio. I have always trusted the Finnish Broadcasting Company's Radio One, and in Arvi Lind's time the television.

Nowadays the newborn and the down-and-outs in the concrete suburbs have everything they need. As does the old codger from Middle Finland in the rehabilitation hospital bed.

I asked the civilised youth which picture I should press to get to the news.

'You shouldn't press the screen,' he said, moving my forefinger quite gently over the lap-computer's screen. 'Just touch it lightly.'

No longer did I have to quarrel with the cyclist. Under the blanket, I watched past and future news bulletins, and

I found all sorts of documentaries there too. For example, about Helmut Kohl, who let himself put on weight but took the unification of Germany seriously. In that job he got a bit thinner, too. I also watched the Romanian revolution, which I had already seen once. Sometimes it was Kari Toivonen reading the news, and then Arvi Lind again.

People in quilted jackets took the fur-hatted dictator and his wife by tank to a cellar somewhere. There they held a trial about the length of a housing co-operative meeting, after which the evil man and his wife were butchered in the backyard. Then they announced that freedom had won. Now we know that the former holders of power jumped from the party's important chairs to the important chairs of big business and ordinary people didn't get much more butter for their porridge.

After Romania I ended up listening to the wartime president Risto Ryti giving a speech after the war. Things didn't go well for him, if you compare him to the cavalry dandy C.G. Mannerheim who puffed away at his cigar in Switzerland while Risto had to endure a war crimes trial. It sure is unfair that the real instigators of the war condemned a peaceful lawyer to prison, where he lost his health. That began to depress me, so I touched the screen to go onwards in history.

I found the European athletics championships from 'Seventy-one. Anssi Kukkonen commentated in such a way that a tear came to my eye even though I did

everything I could to stop it. The stadium was full
of people, like a saucepan absolutely crammed with
potatoes.

'I don't believe in sport,' the cyclist said.

I set the lap television up so that we could both see it.
I told him to watch Jürgen Haase and Juha Väätäinen
running the back straight as if the devil himself were at
their heels. Anyone who doesn't get excited by that is
a creature without feeling. I noticed that lap by lap the
cyclist empathised more with the running, and finally
the nurse came to see what all the yelling in room three
was about. She remembered the same race; she had
been a Soviet citizen then, although she considered
herself more a Lithuanian. She said she had supported
the Finn because he had a glow in his eyes that was
different from anyone else's. I told her that afterwards
it was booze that had made those eyes glow, but I was
ready to forgive him.

One evening the civilised youth told me about some kind
of map service. I sure do have a road map of Finland
in the Escort, from 'Ninety-five; we manage with that.
Whenever a road alignment changes, I mark it with a
pencil.

'I don't doubt it for a moment, but take a look at this.'

The screen showed my home street. I asked when
he had been to photograph it and whether my son was
on the other end of the phone line again. The civilised
youth told me about a computer company that takes

pictures of all the roads in the world and copies all the books. Why has it gone and done something like that? He suspected the reason was increasing advertising revenues, but in his opinion this was irrelevant. The most important thing was that I would be able to travel while I was in my hospital bed.

The picture zoomed in on our house with the back of the Escort visible in the garage, but the number plate was blurred. I had my doubts about that, although I suppose it was OK, like the aerial photographs of your own house plot that were sold during the Seventies.

Pressing the arrow, I took myself on a journey around my home village.

The season was different from now, but they were not very old pictures, because on one electrical transformer cabinet there was a 'Jesus is coming' sticker that had been put there only three summers ago. The civilised youth showed me where he lived, his mother's block of flats and his father's house.

In the evening he went home and I went travelling abroad.

I asked the cyclist, who was in bed reading a thick, foreign-language book, to pick a town. Any town.

'Errr, Vladivostock.'

In Russia the chimneys have red and white stripes; I really have no idea why. They don't pave their streets and under the asphalt plants flower. According to Yrjänä the fault lay not in the country's citizens but in its size. It's easy, after all, for us to keep this small place of our own in better order.

I asked the cyclist to name another town.

'Forssa.'

Forssa had wider streets compared to Russia, and the motorists had stopped at the red lights. Perhaps, though, I would rather visit Vladivostock than Forssa. The cyclist said he had always dreamed of a trip to Forssa, but now he would be happy if he were able to walk on his own two feet from the hospital door to Töölönlahti bay.

I was drawn to even bigger towns. The ones I read about as a child in the children's encyclopaedia: New York, Hong Kong and Buenos Aires.

After dinner I popped over to Jerusalem and Shanghai. You could see from the number of skyscrapers that those Chinese boys had got a good income from the factories that moved there from Europe. One thing I noticed was that the colour and light of the world is completely different in different places. Many of the plants are the same, for example in Jerusalem, where on some hillock there were clearly pines and spruces, but more slender. They have to survive on less water than in Middle Finland, let alone the rainforests.

I fell asleep before I got to the world's northernmost town, in the country of Norway.

Always put your helmet on

I had just come back from the Faroe Islands when a
Zimmer-frame was brought to my bed. I looked at it
and I looked at the doctor and the nurse. I asked if
I looked like a man who needed one of those?

'You're a sporting man,' the doctor said. 'Let's think
of this as a training session.'

Let's think of this as my life. I'm not a Zimmer-frame
man, not at all. I asked whether the doctor had ever
been to the Faroe Islands.

'That's not the subject today.'

Where are the subjects of the day specified? I have
permission to talk about what I want to and today
I want to think about the Faroe Islands and other
distant places. Today you can go a long way cheaply.
A train journey to Pieksämäki costs more than a

weekend break to the Balkans. Today the world is familiar to everyone, but our own country is strange. I'm not complaining, I'm just saying what the world is like.

'There's a simple locking system,' the nurse showed me, pressing some kind of hand-brake on and off.

They weren't listening to me; they didn't understand me at all. I will certainly walk under my own steam or not at all.

There was only one alternative, and it had to succeed. I told the doctor that I was now taking a self-treatment measure and that anyone who was not needed should leave the room. They stayed there as if on guard. I did the same in 'Fifty-eight when my disc swelled up and in 'Seventy-seven when my back was hunched for three weeks after casting a floor.

I pulled myself up against the wall and put the palm of my hand behind my back. I squeezed it into a fist; it now had considerable power. I checked a couple of times to ensure that my lower back was correctly positioned against my knuckles. Then I moved all my weight on top of the knuckle so that my knuckles pressed a little above my buttocks and to the left of my lowest vertebra. I must have grimaced and yelled; that's what I'd done on the previous occasions, anyway. I repeated the movement a couple of dozen times. It hurt a lot; tears flowed from my eyes.

I stopped the doctor from intervening with my free hand. My back crunched, but it helped, as it always did. I managed to drag my legs so that I could sit on the side of the bed. Then I swung them, found my knees and was able to flex my ankles. I promised the doctor that we could try the same thing with the cyclist. My crunching treatment was considerably quicker and cheaper than long-term physiotherapy.

'I certainly think it will be wisest . . .' the doctor stammered.

To go. Away from here.

I took out the lap-computer and wrote a message to my grandchildren. I wrote that Grandpa was fine and in the summer they could come again to eat berries straight from the bush. I packed my black suit in one plastic bag and my other things in another and asked one of the nurses to telephone my son and tell him to come for me.

I hadn't yet left the room when my son Hessu was standing in the doorway. He had something important to say. I always know that's the case when he can't get a word out of his mouth. Three times I had to ask him to cough up what it was that was bothering him.

'Errm . . . care.'

It sure is worth arranging day care for children in good time these days. In my youth they stayed at home, where there were wives to look after them or to have them help knead dough. Or they went to the fields, where there were always menfolk to put a fork in their hands.

'There are different levels of care. For people who can't live at home . . .'

I promised to help my son. I think I'm able to look at these things from a different angle, more of a construction viewpoint. Were the foundations laid in the correct decade and is there enough ventilation if there are five, ten or fifteen children at the nursery.

'I'm not talking about a nursery or early-years education, but . . .'

I asked if he had my will and the fountain pen. He began to rummage for them in his shoulder bag, which has all sorts of badges on it. One is like the Mercedes logo, although according to him it's the peace sign. To me the sign of peace is silence and fresh coffee. And if he came in the Escort then could I have the keys, please.

'No, well . . . I had it tested. And it didn't get its MOT certificate . . .'

Why on earth not?

'It hadn't been inspected for three years.'

Well, of course not. I can't, since I don't have a driving licence.

'You don't have a licence? And you still drive a car?'

Shorter journeys, ones where you can take forest roads. You don't get into dangerous situations when you keep your average speed to fifty-five.

Our conversation died.

My son looked at the watch that wasn't on his wrist, and at his phone.

It sure has always bothered me that my son doesn't think anything like I do. How much easier the world would be if everyone thought like me. Although that's where the problems start, from us thinking that other people are like us. Then we flare up when we realise they aren't. Kolehmainen, the Serbs, the Albanians, our own children or my wife.

My son didn't let me out of the door with my bags. For some reason he was joined by my daughter-in-law, the doctor and even my grandchildren. I could see straight away that the adults were on the same side in their plans, but the children did not know which group they belonged to. My youngest grandchild came up to me and took me by the hand; it would be easier to listen to their stupidity if there were two of us.

The doctor showed my medical notes to my son and daughter-in-law. Then she turned in my direction and said that she had consulted my relatives about all sorts of things. I had to ask her to repeat what she said in Finnish.

'It's decided,' my daughter-in-law said.

I asked whether my daughter-in-law meant that they would keep the baby.

'A place in a care home,' my son faltered. 'We are all of the opinion that it is best to make this decision while you are still in this state . . .'

All of you? Who is it that belongs to this allness? Did anyone ask me?

'The council will pay for part of it; then we will sell some forest.'

You'll sell my forest? Your father's and your grandfather's and your great-grandfather's forest? You certainly will not!

'Of course we don't want this to be done against your will,' the doctor interjected.

What is it that might be done against my will?

'A directive to put you into care.'

I have been in care for many days and now I am directing myself home. Things have an order of priority. It goes like this: feed my wife. Watch the news. Make sure the coffee-maker is switched off. Go to sleep in your own bed.

'There's a thirty-square-metre room,' my son said. 'Mäntylampi, it's called. A private place. I'm sure you remember it.'

Of course I remember it, I've always given it a wide berth because at that time architects designed pointless decorated corners for every building. I told him to listen while a wiser person talked.

We sure should live under the same roof so that we could look after each other and not stuff each generation in turn into a care home. That's what we did in the old days, when there wasn't an alternative. Aunt Ruona had to be endured, even though she ordered you about, smelled bad and used foul language. Now medical science and the calculation of protein percentages have developed so far that there are not enough care home staff. A care home is no place for tender loving care and attention, but an institution for keeping people alive.

Close relatives want to get awkwardly ageing old men and women out of their sight because they cannot stand the worry and fear in their own heads. That's what you do with your children, too. Put them in helmets because you're afraid your child may take a blow to the head. Even though that blow is exactly what's needed to learn how not to get injured.

And now grown-up people don't dare have a child because they are too old. Apparently you would have to give up something in your lives even though it's full of nothing but freedom. You sure are healthy people, and as far as I can see you still have rings on your wedding fingers. In that case you should keep your offspring and not throw them in the bin.

I'll come and look after it. Let's make a care home at your house. I sure haven't taken children in my lap very often, but why shouldn't I learn how, since I've learned hugging from the television?

My son glanced at my daughter-in-law and after that the tears began to flow from his eyes. I had hoped he would have been able to keep his emotions inside as my daughter-in-law did. But if they had made their decision could they please tell me. It would affect my will, too.

The doctor wondered what our conversation had moved on to now. I told the woman to clear off from this meeting of healthy people and go and look after someone who really was sick. The cyclist, for example, they could occasionally ask him how he was feeling.

Not just how the broken back was doing. Do I have to train the doctors in doctor-patient relationships?

I asked my daughter-in-law to think about a couple of things: one day they would be taking her, too, to the old people's home. At that point it could be important that what was now perhaps growing in her from a foetus to a person able to decide matters for him or herself could come to her aid and save the rest of the family from arbitrary decisions. And by the way, I sure remembered what I said on my first ambulance trip. And I remember, too, that my daughter-in-law listened, and believed me. Didn't you?

I have done everything to make sure I am not at the mercy of others.

'For your own good, Dad.'

For your own good, wimps.

Sofa and stool

The ward's doorbell rang and the cab driver stepped inside. I grabbed my things and wished everyone happy days. The cyclist greeted me by lifting his forefinger and little finger into the air. To be on the safe side, I fetched a walking stick from the equipment cupboard, in case I needed it for support. At home I would carve a better one from a suitably curved pine branch.

My son set off after me and said he wanted to come too. When we reached the car, the driver counted us and counted the number of seats in the car.

'There are six of you. I can only take four. I'm sorry, but it's the rules.'

Rules didn't interest me in this situation. My son had reinvented them when he had applied to the care home without asking me. I said I trusted in the driver's ability to drive a German luxury car and in my own ability to hold a child on my lap. It was unnecessary to count the number of safety belts. I pushed my son into the front seat of the taxi and sat down on the back seat with my granddaughter.

The driver shrugged his shoulders and asked if I would pay any possible fine. I said I was on my way home and the fine would be divided equally between the three adults in the car. My son intervened and said our destination was the care home.

I corrected him, saying that our destination was number fifteen, Jokivarrentie road. In my son's opinion that was quite a long way from the care home, but I urged the driver simply to start the engine and find the motorway. The driver glanced at me through the mirror, alternately, a couple of times, as if checking the chain of command.

'Moteway, moteway.'

I asked whether the driver was from maybe Tampere or somewhere around Leningrad, as I could distinguish an unusual note in his speech. The man said he was from Narva and explained what part of Estonia it was in.

I've been on a trip on the Helsinki-Tallinn ferry in my time, with the smallholder lads. We were loaded into buses at the harbour and taken to look at a farm where the cow with the greatest yield of milk in the Baltic lived. When you looked closely at that cow you could see immediately that the locals lived in poverty and not a drop of that milk went to them.

I went to Estonia another time after they got their own flag and money and began to have their own sportsmen and not just a bankrobber named Raivo. My wife and I went to some spa in the old, stone-built city, where I refused to have a mud bath or to allow strange ladies to massage my neck and, more particularly, to buy the Red Army peaked caps that were on sale in the cobbled streets. The Bolsheviks caused such a lot of harm in a short time that their caps have no place in my home, any more than the cap of an SS officer.

The man from Narva asked if he could play a CD because he was trying to learn Finnish as he drove. I gave permission, expecting some kind of language cassette, but instead I heard the voice of a gruff Olympic champion.

I would have sung along, if I could sing. From the car speakers came a tune about Anttila rising from his bed, then it was the 'Wanderer's Waltz' and 'Sunshine and the Fairy'. The man from Narva could sing all of them with about eighty-seven per cent grammatical accuracy. At the end of 'Sunshine', I noticed my daughter-in-law wiping her cheek. I don't know if she was crying because of the song or the situation or tiredness. When she was tired my wife sometimes shed tears without even noticing.

I asked the driver what it felt like to be so far away from home, taking an unknown family to Middle Finland and listening to Tapio Rautavaara. There must be decent singing and talking companions in his home country too.

The man from Narva shrugged his shoulders in a way that suggested he didn't want to think about his answer too much.

A person sure should be allowed to be in his own home.

'My home stays where it is,' he said. 'Two months work here, two weeks at home.'

When he had enough money, he planned to set up his own transport business in Estonia. A lot of clients came from Finland, and he would be able to arrange all sorts of trips for them. At the moment it was more difficult because of the recession, and more was demanded both of equipment and entertainment. It was no longer enough to offer booze and mud treatments as inducements.

The man from Narva had three children, whose pictures were on the sun visor, and two grandchildren. He didn't have a picture of his wife, or else he didn't want to show us one. I nodded as a sign of understanding; you couldn't say anything to that.

We drove through a built-up area, through scattered settlements and field-edges, the middles of forests in a companionable silence. In the background, time after time, Rautavaara interpreted his own and Helismaa's verses, songs and ballads.

At the Puropaju crossroads I asked the driver to make a detour via my home.

'Hey, Dad . . . we were supposed to go to the Mäntylampi care home . . . more or less directly.'

A person is allowed to fetch what he needs from his home.

'OK. Clothes and such? A toothbrush maybe. Medicines?'

I asked the driver to park so that the headlights shone straight into the workshop. My smaller grandchild had fallen asleep on the back seat; the car always does that, I suppose it's like their mother's lap or womb. I leaned on the walking stick because in heavy autumn rain the yard can be quite muddy. I asked my son to come and help me.

At one corner of the coffin the wood had split, but it only made it look better, just as a scar can make a too beautiful man more handsome. My son stayed behind by the door, picking something up from the floor.

'Dad. What are these?'

Surely a person can recognise a photograph. Put them away and come and help me.

'Why's the head missing?'

Who from?

'All of them, really.'

I took the photographs in my hand; they had been taken by my wife. I remember how funny they looked when she had them developed. Somehow my wife hadn't completely understood how the viewfinder worked. Sometimes the subject was missing a head, a hand or the new jeans my son had asked her to photograph.

'It sure is quite cool, the era of film,' my son mused. 'You saw your mistakes. Now you can delete them straightaway if you don't like them.'

That was the difference between the world in the old days and now. But there were some ugly colours in the days when colour photographs were new.

My son didn't dispute my view. He collected the photographs into a bundle, tidied the pile and went on looking at the pictures. I asked whether he intended to let the taxi meter go on running.

'This looks familiar. When was it taken, do you remember?'

I sure did remember. And I remember who took it. My son himself.

We're standing on the outside steps and waving at him. Or, more accurately, my wife is waving, I'm looking at the gutter to see if it's dripping water. That was the day when my son moved away from home to his university town and when the car pulled away, my wife and I were left, the two of us alone in the house for the first time in quite a few decades. I told my wife I would go on with my jobs. She put on her apron and went to do the dishes. In the evening she thought it was much too quiet, although for the past twenty years there had been far too much din as the children learned to be people. I solved the problem by turning up the television. In my wife's opinion that was the wrong way to cope with loneliness, although it worked for me. More often than not my wife was right.

'Yes . . . yeah,' my son commented, as he didn't know what else to say, and put the pictures where I told him to. Finally he came to help me. We lifted the lid on to the coffin and I pulled a tarpaulin across to protect it. I told my son that he would find the trailer behind the woodshed, one man sure would be able to pull it by hand.

'What do I need a trailer for? I've never driven with a trailer.'

I said I would explain in more detail in my will. Now I wanted to reveal to my son something to which I had devoted a lot of time and all my skill. I pulled the sheet off my work like a portrait sculptor. I asked my son for his opinion.

'Errm . . .'

That was a strange opinion.

'What is it?'

It's a wooden grave marker.

How is it that no one before me has had the idea of making a wooden grave marker? Wood is closer to the earth, and warmer, than a piece of granite. Wood is warm, living and important to us Finns.

'Strange.'

An aeroplane is strange, the Danish language is strange and yeah-yeah-yeah music videos are strange. There is nothing strange about a wooden grave marker.

'I think it's strange, although I don't mean to say that . . . there's anything . . . well, bad about it. Strange can be good. Do you know, for example, there's a lot of atonal music that is just like, you know . . .'

I said I had settled on wood so that the villagers would whisper. This is what they would whisper: such an ordinary person he was, but look how handsomely he could carve wood.

'Well, perhaps if you look at it from that perspective,' my son explained. 'It does have soul.'

Well, there's no soul, even in people, but I didn't feel like going on discussing the matter with my son. I still had to discuss the grave marker with the minister, but that could wait until tomorrow. There was someone new in Lempiäinen's job.

I told my son to lift the piece of wood on to the wheelbarrow, and we used this to take it to the boot of the taxi. In the dark garden I could see the taxi's dim interior light as well as my daughter-in-law, who was following with interest what we were bringing to the car. We lifted the grave marker into the boot and after that I went inside to fetch milk and hunter's sausage from the fridge, Edam cheese and berries from the freezer, as well as a block of ice cream for the children.

As we continued on our way, Tapio's disc played 'Deck of Cards'. The man from Narva played it twice because he felt the articulation was particularly clear. After a moment's silence he said his car had four wheels, like the number of seasons in the year. We all found that funny.

My son told the driver to turn left immediately after the sports field, but actually the correct route was right at the petrol pump. The driver obeyed me and my son was left to shake his head in disappointment. He wondered why we were going to Jokivarrentie road: no one we knew lived there, all there was there was a block of flats and a dog-exercise park. I told the man from Narva to reverse up to the main door so that we could lift the grave marker straight into the vestibule and from there into the chicken coop in the cellar.

I paid the man from Narva with five smooth notes and refused to take the credit card my daughter-in-law tried to foist on me.

'Where is it that we're going?' my son said. 'This is the wrong building. An ordinary block of flats.'

I held my grandchildren between me and my son and daughter-in-law.

There was a numerical code for the main door, but I preferred to use a key. And anyway, you can trust the people of your own village enough not to have to use keys or codes. If you lock the door, some lowlife will immediately get the idea that there is something that is worth keeping behind lock and key. Olympics money, a valuable piece of crocheting or a copper tube.

At home I don't have anything that is valuable to anyone but me.

My son wondered why I had the keys to a strange block of flats. Did someone we knew live here? I said I knew the constructor, we had worked on the same jobs in the early Eighties and for that reason, during the building project, he let me go a few times to see how young people set one brick on top of another.

I only had to show them a couple of times, they sure were competent workmen, some of them from the same country as the man from Narva.

I climbed the stairs with my smallest grandchild, because I needed support for my leg. We got as far as the third floor before the lift arrived with the others. I opened the door of flat A12.

'How come you have the key to this place?' my son asked. 'What is this place? Surely there isn't anything here?'

Sofa and stool were certainly in their own places. One on the back wall of the living room and the other in the north-east corner. I prompted my daughter-in-law to plug the fridge into the wall and unload the food from the middle cardboard box.

'Sofa and stool? Errm . . . how did you know there was a sofa and a stool here?'

Because I made them. I was also going to make a dresser, a kitchen table and bunk beds for my grandchildren, but then my wife got sick and the job remained unfinished.

'Why did you bring the sofa and stool you made here?'

Have we gone we completely mad? Because everyone's home should have a sofa and a stool, of course.

'What do you mean? Whose home?'

How many times do I have to say it? Do we need to go to the health centre to get your ears syringed like when you were a little boy? My daughter-in-law showed more understanding, praising the view and the size of the rooms, saying there was plenty of space, how many square metres?

Sixty-two. Calculated for two people.

My smallest granddaughter made some sounds in the empty bedroom and liked the echo a lot. My son worried that the neighbours might hear. They sure wouldn't, because the downstairs flat was in a probate sale and Sintonen upstairs hadn't heard anything since 'Eighty-five.

My wife and I were supposed to move into the flat when my wife told me that she couldn't rake, dig potatoes, pick berries or wade through the snow to the sauna, which didn't have warm water. I did the deal when the construction of the block of flats began. The deposit was in our bank account, and I raised the rest by selling forest. I didn't need anything from the bank; there would be many decades to recoup the investment.

But I never got the chance to tell my wife that the apartment was waiting for us. I was waiting for the right day. The more I waited, the more awkward it got. I was worried that my wife would be too excited about something that didn't excite me. I was afraid that there would be a removal van in the yard the very next day.

I thought, one more spring and one more autumn at home.

But springs, autumns, summers, winters and mud seasons went by and always we raked, always we dug potatoes, because home was home.

I know now what the matter was. I was scared of moving into town. I knew that my wife would be fine; she would go to Inkeri's café and to Inkeri's sister Inari's hairdressing salon. She would leaf through the women's magazines and listen to gossip and she would enjoy the easy life without sweat, hard work and cold.

Often I managed to say to my wife, listen, what if we . . .

But I never got any further, because I didn't want to move out of my own home. Did I really want to have a sauna which heats at the touch of a button? Where the water comes straight from the tap and burns your fingers. Where the distance to the bank, the kiosk, the church or the kebab place is so short that you could crawl or toddle? Would I forget the taste of potato and want a double kebab in soft bread every day and let myself put on weight?

'This is your flat . . .' my son finally understood.

Slowly as an energy-saving bulb it dawned on him. It was the same in school running races; he always gave the others a ten-metre start.

I sent my son and my daughter-in-law to the cellar to fetch mattresses and bedclothes. I thought I would watch the evening news on the lap television while they were busy, but it had become a children's toy. They were shooting some kind of birds in the air with a sling-shot. The game particularly amused the smallest of the children; she could control the device as easily as

I handled a hammer and nails. When I was their age, I don't even think I knew about things like electricity.

I sat on the stool to look into the darkness in which the light of the lap television gleamed. It lit up the three children's faces; I could hear the sound of the game. Somehow it made me want to laugh. It was a different kind of feeling.

Judas

I made some coffee and jolted my son awake. I told
him not to wake the others, but showed him the
changes I had made to the flat. Safety rails, non-slip
mat, and I'd ensured that the cutting board, dining
table and coffee machine were at the right height for
my wife. I could never have imagined that my wife
would be the first of us to leave the coffee-making
place. Now, of course, it's a bit low for me.

My son found himself a coffee cup, adding some
milk and too much sugar.

'Dad . . . this, errm, these doings with death . . .
what's it all about?' he whispered. 'You know, I've read
about depression in the elderly. I took copies at the
university, printed out relevant pages. If you wanted to
read them.'

I said I had made ready, just as a sensible person prepares his summer cabin for the winter. Clears the gutters, repairs rust patches, replaces rotting timbers. Insulates the water pipes so that they won't freeze with the first frost. It's no different to that.

The lights by the riverside had stayed on throughout the night. I have my doubts as to whether it's worth lighting up the river. It has flowed in the same channel through the Stone Age and the Ice Age, and moonlight has always been enough. A fish can see to swim in the darkness and the homeless people would also sleep better if it wasn't always as bright as in a prison cell. I know one of them, we were in the same class at school and we went to the army in consecutive age classes. Surukainen must be the longest-lived wino in this country.

'Will you listen to what I'm trying to say?' my son whispered.

I said I wasn't intending to make his life, or mine, any more difficult.

'I'm . . . we're on the same page. The intention is to make both our lives easier. Yours and ours.'

Let's halve the problem. I move to town, to this flat, which is designed for elderly people, and definitely safe. I will even wear a helmet, if it makes you happy. But. At weekends I will go to my own home and want to be left alone.

My son looked at me. I noticed that my daughter-in-law, on her sofa, was also awake. They looked at each

other. I said that I could always call on my neighbour,
Kolehmainen, and soon their son would also be able to
come and knock on my door to see if I was still alive.
I had on my travels also met a civilised youth who would
definitely be coming to visit me, and in him I would
have a scribe to record my memoirs. I had researched
on-demand printing on the computer; when they were
ready I would be able to print an edition of eight copies.

'What shall I say to Mäntylampi? The care home?
It wasn't easy to get you a place.'

Tell them there's one bed free for someone who needs
it; I'm sure there will be plenty of applicants.

Then I shook hands with my son, shook hands with
my daughter-in-law. She hugged me, slightly against my
will, before I managed to set off to meet the minister.

Our town's church was built in 1876. The trees were
felled from our own forests. Or from the forests that
people claimed were theirs, since the church owns the
best mixed forest this side of the Puropaju border.
The church bells were cast in Stockholm. The poor-
man collecting box stands in front of the belfry. I have
given money, and all my lunch vouchers too, when
they began to give us those on top of our pay packets,
pushing them through the poor-man's slot.

I climbed calmly up the steps, one at a time, and
examined the church's walls. The paintwork of our
village's most important building sure was in poor
condition, and moss was growing on the stone steps.

What would a townie driving through our village think, when the first thing they saw was the sports ground, whose rubber asphalt surface is torn, and then the church, which looks abandoned by God and man? I pulled at the church door, but it did not move. Either it had become dozens of kilos heavier or the power of my arms had lessened in this fight.

After a moment a young woman leaped up the eight church steps, smiling so broadly that I did not know if this was appropriate on church property. I nodded calmly back at her and stepped in through the door she opened. I asked whether this was the new fashion among today's youth? That they no longer go straight to the shower, the swimming pool or the lake, but come to cleanse themselves through prayer?

'I run here every day. Just the right distance, seven kilometres, and such incredibly beautiful views.'

I walked forward along the aisle. I said I had been here in the Forties doing voluntary work when the positions of two windows were changed. I sure don't remember why, but the altar piece was lifted carefully from its place by fourteen men.

'That's very interesting.'

Actually, it was pretty stupid. Two men to do the lifting would have been enough. The painters of altar pieces are always remembered, but the painters of the inside and outside walls of churches are recalled less often. There is a lot of talk of Gallen-Kallela and Michelangelo, but what about Oiva Ruohoranta, who always did good work and never questioned even the stupidest colour choices on the part of the client? There really is more holiness in an even layer of red ochre than in a picture of a saviour with a gleaming head raising a sick man from the dead.

'We should remember those whom we forget,' the young woman said. 'It is easy to remember those who are always before our eyes, or who are louder than the rest.'

I gazed at the altar piece, which showed all the disciples apart from Judas. Of all the people in the big book, it is him I have thought about most. He sure has been dogged by an unnecessarily bad reputation. What would have become of Jesus of Nazareth without Judas's hankering for silver coins? He might have led a long and peaceful life as a carpenter and father of eight children.

'Maybe.'

He would definitely have let himself get fat.

'I hardly think so.'

He would have been just like anyone else. He would have looked back at his life and thought, I had very heated opinions when I was a young man, and the desire to change the whole world's way of thinking to my own. His lovely wife would have made Jesus a cup of strong coffee and they would have gone to Gethsemane for a Sunday walk. They would have had those eight children. So everyone who believes in Jesus and the forgiveness of sins should thank Judas.

'That's a big ontological question and a subject for research. After all, he was at the same time a person and the Son of God and God. The doctrine of the trinity . . .'

I continued by saying that I had always wondered about pictures of the crucifixion. People wear crosses around their necks, even though a cross is the most horrible method of execution possible. If the same story were to be told today, would Jesus the Nazarene sit in an electric chair?

'The cross symbolises, above all, the forgiveness of sins . . .'

The electric chair reminded me of the pulpit; I have always wanted to stand in it. I wondered how many sermons had been preached from it.

'It has its own history; nothing is born from nothing,' said the woman in the tracksuit, and went round the church checking the radiators.

I wondered why it had been necessary to switch to radiators; at one time there were perfectly good barrel heaters in each corner. The tracksuit woman said she was new here and didn't know much about building technology.

I asked if she knew where I could find the new minister, Lempiäinen. The woman gestured for me to follow her and took me to the minister's office. She showed me an upholstered chair and I asked if I looked as if I didn't have the energy to stand. Because I didn't. The woman smiled benevolently and took her jacket off and wiped the sweat from her forehead with a little towel. Since when did the verger or intern have the same wardrobe as the minister, I wondered.

'I am the minister.'

For a moment, I sure couldn't think of anything to say in response. I had never before seen a woman as minister. There have been women doctors for a long time, and at time of the last forest thinning I even saw one driving a forest machine, and there are policewomen, but I have seen women ministers only on the television. Of course, it is a very good job for a woman, like that of a politician or a telephone salesperson, since it is based on persuading and convincing people through the spoken word.

I wanted to get to the point and said I had come to talk about my funeral. I looked in my trouser pocket for my list of music.

'You have some requests for hymns? I am sure it is wise to go through this in advance . . . no one has done it before . . . Do you have some favourite hymn that you sang as a child?'

Even as child, I would have preferred not to sing. My voice is bad, and I can only find rhythm when I am splitting logs. There is one good hymn, the one that says 'Lord in your hand may I live', even though I sure don't understand how anyone could fit into the palm of someone's hand.

The minister lady listened, writing things down on a yellow Post-it note. To begin, Jaakko Teppo's 'Hilma and Onni', which I have always wanted to hear played on the organ, accompanied by the civilised youth's violin. After that an accordionist could play Harri Klusila's instrumental version of 'My Heart of Winter Stayed on Ice'. And then one of Tapio Rautavaara's pieces, as long as it is not the one that bemoans the marks left by one's own beer mugs.

The menu.

The basic things need to be in order: Karelian hot-pot, boiled potatoes and root beer. And Karelian pasties with egg-butter. No grated vegetables or dill pickles. No tofu or sprouts. A big coffee-pot, whole milk. The minister lady said that she was not in charge of the catering side, that it would be worth my while to get competitive estimates from the village's two businesses. I sure haven't ever made people compete, except when we got the children to see who could empty their plate the quickest.

But there should be one table for the young people and another for seekers after the exotic: we should offer a Thai version of Karelian hot-pot and kebab sauce from a squeezy bottle. For meat-refusers, salad, cucumber, tomatoes, turnips and boiled frankfurters. There should also be a Christmas ham and some home-made mustard. The home can be anyone's.

Dessert.

Pancakes with strawberry jam or sugar. No ice cream, because it's no time until it melts in your lap. They can make them outside in a frying pan.

When we'd talked about the food, I asked the
minister lady to follow me to the churchyard. We
would look at where my earthly remains would be
interred. The minister lady said she was busy, but she
had enough manners not to run away from something
of importance to an old person.

I showed her the plot that belonged to my wife and
me, beside my mother and father's grave. The grave
marker was under a towel, waiting in the shade of a
tree. I dug a little of the lawn and the sandy earth away
with the heel of my boot and set the piece of timber
in its place. The minister lady examined the surface of
the wood, running her fingers along the grain of the
timbers.

'Amazing. This is almost like a work of art, you sure
are talented.'

Three times in my life I have chuckled. This was the
fourth.

I promised to let her have the design for the grave
marker; she could have it mass produced if she wanted
to, since I may run out of time. It would surely be of
use around the world, for poor families and rich seekers
after the exotic. If they were to be exported to our
eastern neighbour, all you would need to do was cover
the wooden surface in gold leaf.

'What is your name? I would like to use our
conversation in my sermon, with your permission. You
have given me some formidable perspectives on change,
which today is more frenzied than perhaps ever before

in the history of mankind. The encounter of new and old. But also the fact that in the end nothing between people really changes.'

I told her my name, but forbade her to mention it to the congregation. The villagers could recognise me by the context, and anyway, I didn't think that people really went to church any more.

'Every parishioner is important. Every person is a potential parishioner.'

It was clearer in the old days. Every Sunday the congregation came to the big church, from children to stooped old women and men, because they had to. No one listened to the sermon, but it was nice to see new faces and to travel by horse and cart. Your clothes pinched, and mother combed your hair many times. Nowadays there are road churches and shopping centre churches where attempts are made to get people to stop for a moment.

'There have been successes, too,' the woman said. 'We just have to go where people go.'

I can tell you: there haven't. You don't.

The world is the same, as good or as bad as it has been for the past 2,000 years. But people have changed. They do not need God, because in the department stores, products are God. On the road speed is God. At the motorway service station, better loos and filled rolls.

'You bear strong witness,' the woman said. 'And you are not entirely wrong, either.'

My peaceful place is after the Ojala fields, where the ancient woodland begins but in spring you can already hear the burbling of the brook. In winter, snow falls from the branches and in autumn the colours change at terrific speed to red and then yellow and grey.

'God is everywhere.'

Or else He is nowhere.

Katri Helena

The minister lady and I were heading in the same direction. She was going to the health centre's ward day-room to prepare for communion; I walked to my wife's room to see how things were going. My son, my daughter-in-law and my grandchildren were already there. My youngest granddaughter was chatting to my wife's room-mate about horses. Both thought horses were lovely.

My oldest grandchild was sitting on a chair a little further away. At that age it is hard to watch someone who has been strong become old, weak and frail. Weakness is frightening because you do not want it for yourself. It is only when you begin to get closer to being bedridden yourself that you begin to accept the only thing that is real about life. I would have liked to help the girl, but that is a lesson only life can teach.

I took a chair and sat beside my wife. I asked my son whether he had already fed her her morning porridge; he nodded but said that he had left giving her coffee to me. I let my wife sip from a sippy mug and whispered that I had been here and there, as I had when I was a young man.

I fell out of a coffin.

I had to go to hospital.

I got a lap television.

I moved into town.

I met the minister lady.

Then I glanced at my son and said that in addition to the television we might soon be welcoming into our arms a completely new person, but that they weren't saying anything. My wife swallowed her coffee; I crumbled a sugar lump in the palm of my hand and placed small pieces on her tongue.

I set the cup down on her bedside cabinet and took out the lap television. I showed my wife a few pictures of the coffin, the grave marker and finally the Jokivarrentie road flat in the light of morning. I apologised that there were quite a few more things that I had never managed to tell her about.

My wife may have nodded a bit, or maybe she just wanted some more coffee. I asked whether my wife knew that our minister was a woman and much less frightening than the minister who had married us. Paavali Samuel Hermunen. Hearing his name made my wife laugh.

After coffee we lifted my wife into a sitting position in her wheelchair. I told her that I had gone rally driving with our granddaughter in one like it in the country's biggest hospital.

Anneli was able to get to the day room by herself, accompanied by the nurse and my middle grandchild. The girl said she was looking after a foal that was named after her at the Tuomarinkylä stables every week. Anneli said that her father had six working horses and one show horse, the only one in Viipuri and with a fine French name to boot.

I pushed my wife's chair into position and sat down a little farther away from the ceremony, in an armchair that had been set in front of the television. I picked up a magazine from the table, but really I was listening to the minister lady's hymn-singing. I remembered what a pretty voice my wife had when she thought she was alone in the kitchen or the barn humming along with the radio to the singer Katri Helena.

The little I could hear of the sermon with my better ear was about the meeting between me and the minister lady. Young people are able to clothe their thoughts in words quickly. The minister lady said something about old people being resources and new ways of looking at things that they, the younger ones, did not understand. I waited to see if she would say anything about Finland's only wooden grave marker, but perhaps she was leaving it for her next sermon.

My son came to sit by me.

He took the other *Seura* magazine. The grandchildren also came to sit in the television corner, so that it looked as if it was our home, only there was a communion service in progress in the back part of our living room.

The minister lady began to distribute wafers and a red drink which I hoped was not wine. Many of the patients were on medications that meant things could have got noisy after just one gulp.

At the same time Risto Lipponen ambled up to us with a sly expression on his face. He had pissed his pants again, but that didn't bother Risto. He said he had no intention of participating in the religious knowledge lesson over there, or in the algebra one that came next, but to escape to Mäkelänvuori. I asked why there. Risto Lipponen said you could see as far as the island if you used binoculars. And what was there on the island? Girls from the sports club swimming completely naked. After that Risto Lipponen winked at me and continued on his way. I winked back.

I thought, so this is what today has been like. How could a day be any different from what it is?

P.S.

Will
   I myself thus declare my last will and testament to be that my property should be divided after my death as follows.

1.
My property namely my Home shall go to my grandchildren. We know what my own children would do: sell it off or let it rot.

   You will look after the taxes and other outgoings and keep the house painted and the shed in order. Resources for this will be arranged as specified in paragraph 2. If the oak tree in the garden rots, you will fell it and plant a new one. You will take the children with you and if it is absolutely necessary you are permitted to have them wear helmets. Son: the motor saw will start if you keep it at an angle of thirty-seven degrees, with the blade toward the earth. Plastic components are not to be used, nor mechanical air-conditioning. The womenfolk can look after the garden if they wish.

Men are these days to be counted as women.

My neighbour Kolehmainen's son Jarmo is permitted to use the property during the winter and in summer for the two weeks before Midsummer. You will not argue about the days.

My home will not go to developers or to cabin renters from the south who would leave the place uncleaned and their sausage wrappers in the forest.

I declare: in the walls of that house is my soul, if one may use too big a word for once in one's life. And in the floor and in the potato cellar.

2.

There are forty-eight hectares of forest. I have gradually bought more as people moved away and the parish needed more Finnish markka for its coffers in the Nineties.

You sure may sell ten hectares. Twenty are to be tended as commercial forests are tended. Well, with consideration and profitably. Twenty are to be left in their natural state.

The annual thinning will finance the renovation and maintenance of the house. The electric radiators will be exchanged for geothermal heating in three years' time on Finland's Independence Day.

If my daughters-in-law wish to buy new cars with the forest money, I declare: Japanese cars last, but are small and ugly. German ones do too, but are large and expensive. Be sensible and buy a Ford.

3.

I have hidden banknotes in the cellar. I sure don't remember how much. I put them there for the first time in 'Fifty-eight when it felt as if our neighbour to the east was experiencing a desire to expand again and that the baldie president Urho Kalevi Kekkonen did not have it in him to stop it. Another time I made my own deposit when the Finnish markka was turned into European money. They will be worth looking for on a rainy day. They can no longer be exchanged for valid currency, but it may be that notes like that have value as antiques. At one time there were tens of thousands of them.

4.

There is good money in three accounts. The Finnish Union Bank, the National Share Bank and the Post Office Bank, I don't remember what they're called these days. The passbooks are in the top drawer of the dresser, under my organ donor card. There is a total of something like 106,014 euros. I didn't get it by spending, but by saving. A little put aside from every pay packet, every annual percentage and every pension payment.

You will use the money as follows:

You will pay for my wife's care when the municipal services are closed down. I estimate that this will happen in 2018.

My son knows a good place for my wife, the one you were going to put me in. You will make sure that the bed has a lake view, but is also positioned so that there is some life for her to watch. I will record all the words and articles that make my wife laugh on an audio tape recorder.

Let the contents of the cupboards be divided as follows: half to my direct descendants. The other half to Kolehmainen's son, the civilised youth and the middle- and long-distance racers of the Middle Finland Sports Association. Its contact details are to be found in the notebook with the black cover at home.

The money may not be used for exorbitant living or, definitely not, for pigging out. If you intend to buy shares, then I recommend Middle Finland Tyres or Middle Finland Water. When the roads deteriorate, more tyres will be used all the time. Water, on the other hand, is always as essential as potatoes.

5.
You will visit my wife every week. Without the two of us you would not exist; it's as simple as that.

6.

I donate my collection of Jaakko Teppo records to the library.

7.

Reinikainen's comedy cassettes will go to the taxi driver from Narva. He does not, however, have to adopt the dialect, although it could come in handy if he has fares that take him to the Pirkanmaa region.

8.

My wife's old clothes are in the attic; they will be useful for my daughter-in-law when she puts on a bit of weight.

9.

Kolehmainen: you can keep the circular saw. You can mow our garden once every four years. The rest of the time the grass can be scythed. There will be more butterflies.

10.

The Ford Escort can stay for driving in the yard, the little ones sure will like it. Niilo Tuohinen from Vihtakylä knows where to get spare parts. His telephone number is 5679, at least it was in the Seventies.

11.

The minister lady has my funeral plan, but here are a couple of additional instructions:

Avoid: sanctimoniousness.

It sure is an unpleasant trait in people, at funerals and in politics, that. It's useless to claim how fine a man I was if you don't really think so. You can cry if you have to. Shedding tears for form's sake is forbidden.

If you feel like having a dance, dance. I have seen the funeral of a South African liberator in which people put on bright clothes and threw paper streamers, played drums and dance. Why not grieve joyfully?

12.
Completely forbidden in the church and parish hall: electricity. Including: musical instruments, mixers, microwave ovens, organs, lighting, digital cameras.

13.
Permitted: opinions.

After dessert and coffee, free speech for friends and enemies.

Otherwise it might be like Kurkkainen's young wife, who always humoured and understood her unpleasant mother and her myriad ailments. At her mother's deathbed the young wife exploded. She shouted: I won't miss you at all, you stinking, corpse-like deep-water fish. I will give the house away for nothing. Even at the funeral she was still muttering, by the coffin, it was a good thing I got rid of you, you barren old bird.

Let it all out. Don't worry, I will be halfway to being cow parsley by that stage.

14.

To the minister lady, separately, this advice: the church gutters need seeing to. You can see the rust when you look upwards but not as far as the heavens. Let 1.4 per cent of my savings be reserved for the maintenance of the church building.

15.

Let the coffin be brought to the church in the Ford Escort's trailer, protected by a tarpaulin. If I have time, I will build a couple of benches on the platform.

The material part ends here. Let us move on to the spiritual bequest, which I offer now as follows:

1.

You can get by with plain talking.

2.

Ordinary things are sufficient.

3.

Drink spirits with restraint, preferably not at all.

4.

People are wise and stupid at the same time. It is worth looking at them through many kinds of spectacles. One good thing is to take a photograph and then check a couple of decades later to see if your opinion has changed. From close up you don't always notice all you should.

It gets more complicated. I'm not going to start explaining any more of it. There is a hole in the paper at this point because I used the rubber so much.

Those called together and present at this time thus witness that I myself, whom we personally know, has today in healthy and full understanding and of his own free will declared the above to comprise his last will and testament and that he has at the same time signed this testament in his own hand.

Time and place as aforementioned

Witnesses
Civilised Youth   Kolehmainen, Jarmo

P.S. Daughter-in-law: if you kept the little one, it would be better. If you did, then he or she too will know that he or she is mentioned quite separately in this will. Each of my grandchildren has their own tree marked in the forest, they can look for it with an orienteering map and compass. I left a couple of surprises at the roots of the trees.

P.P.S. In the photograph box you will find some letters which I considered burning, but have changed my mind, as I have often done in recent times. I am sure I am going soft in the head. You can read the letters out loud in the parish hall or wherever you want.

In the attic room, 17.4.1954

My love,

You said you do not say things like that. You don't
need to, because I can. My love. I could write it here
a few more times, but there is a limit to the amount of
sense you can commit to paper. I hope the Pöntiö Town
Hall will be finished soon so that I can have you back.
I hope you will be able to borrow some woolly socks,
because you left yours here, under the bed.

I miss you. You said you don't know how to say that,
either, but are you going to stop me. I miss you.

Of course I am thankful that I can live here in your
father and mother's attic, although sometimes I have
longed for the town. Everything will be clearer when we
are officially engaged and I can wear this beautiful ring.
You can carve incredibly well in wood.

Your mother talks a lot about the wedding. I have thought about it too, waiting and nervous. That brings to mind the third thing that may not be said. The wedding waltz. I'm writing it down once more, even at the risk of us splitting up: the wedding waltz. You will, my old man, dance the wedding waltz.

You were wrong to think I wouldn't get on with your father. It's true he's an old fogey who believes that everything was better in the old days and that you can eat mouldy bread and those born at the end of the Nineteenth century are the only people who remember what life was like when it was still hard enough.

It makes me laugh inside, as he is so serious. Don't worry, I don't say anything to him, even when I see him through the window tilling the potato field with a horse-drawn plough while old Kolehmainen next door uses one of those new tractor things.

Now I'm rambling.

There is something more important.

We're going to have a baby.

(...)

My love,

I'm writing even though I have not yet received a letter from you.

I can feel it already, I know that it exists, I don't need anyone's word or examination. At first I felt sick, that's why I was a bit cross and snappy last time we were in the same room, in the hallway, and you asked if there was something wrong. There is nothing wrong, this is the beginning. I hope you are reading this alone and in peace and not in the middle of a working break and now you will have to keep all this inside you as I know you will.

I will not tell your father, or even your mother, although I feel she guesses something. At the coffee table just now she said I shouldn't be pressed into field work but should stay inside to knead the dough. According to your father a daughter-in-law shouldn't be cosseted or she will start to have ideas and dream of her inheritance. Perhaps it was just a saying. They sure drink a lot of coffee at your house, but that's fine of course, now that rationing has stopped completely.

We will have a good life. So much is possible, peace continues, the weather is favourable; I often feel like singing. I see our house as you drew it on squared paper. I added some cupboard space in the kitchen and the attic should be made inhabitable straight away if we are blessed with more children. I am sure I'm allowed to paint the walls in different colours; I'll do it even if I'm not allowed. Don't you worry about it, the inside walls of the house are my responsibility my love.

I must go, your mother has just said that the dough has risen. Write. There are loaves and buns of all sorts in the oven.

My love. I miss you. Wedding waltz.

Your own R.

7.11.1968

Dear Sir You!

Do you know how long we have gone without speaking? I know: twenty-nine days. Since you don't speak about anything, it's not worth my doing so either. And why? Because I turned up the radiators. There are children in the house, I have my hands full of work, you have your hands full of work. The radiators are there so that we don't need to heat the house with wood any more.

I don't always understand you. I don't have any more words for this. Explaining won't help at all.

I am at my sister's. I will stay here as long as I have to, to let the anger evaporate.

Don't try to reach me. Put enough clothes on the boys and see that they are fed. Boil potatoes.

2009 or whatever year it is now

My pen won't obey me. The words go in the wrong places I hope you are not agnry with me. Agry. Argny. Angry.

I don't remember things.

I am afraid, my love. Remember for me remember the things I have to remember I miss you I don't remember what I miss. What is this? The night is long. I miss you. The night is convex waning sleek

What all should I remember? I did remember a moment ago.

In my bed a strange man, he claims to be you. Old he is; you are young, I do not know him with him I danced the wedding waltz did I

My love

I have relaxed a little

At night I can hear the sounds of mopeds, during the day the neighbour's wife has a coughing attack which will not end until the flag in the garden is flown at half-mast. I think I will go back home, for the summer at the latest.

Another day I think differently.

Sure, so much has never happened outside my window. At home you could see the field in different seasons, the big birch tree, an even bigger birch tree and the forest behind them. All that changed during my eighty years were the generations of squirrels and a few Kolehmainens.

From the balcony of my block of flats at a quarter past five I can see the postman, the taxi driver or the dairy van taking deliveries to the shop milk that is called

Finnish even though it could be shipped in from Narva. The kebab boys arrive at the restaurant after six and remember to say hello to me because they know me as the old codger who stands on high, coffee cup in hand. At seven the long-distance bus service comes to the schoolyard, always the same three children, knapsacks on their backs. Two of them are friends, the third is alone. He will either be a down-and-out or a card-game millionaire; those are the possibilities these days for people who are not allowed to play with the others.

I have loosened up a little, my weight has gone up three hundred grams. That is because on the second Monday of every month I am in the habit of going to Irmeli's Café and Deli. I sure try to do it in such a way that none of the old men of the village notice.

I go to the library every day. I read the *Middle Finland* newspaper, the newspaper of the capital and I look at the pictures in all sorts of foreign papers, because the world begins, on account of the lap computer, to be familiar to me. Another good thing is the swimming baths. I can swim the twenty-five-metre pool from one end to the other without drawing breath even once. I circle the playing field three times and then go straight to Kuusikoti to see my wife.

The same home help seldom comes here twice. The week before last it was a man who was black as night, who spoke Finnish and came from Aänekoski. I made some coffee and offered him some seeded buns I bought from the German shop. All Finnish chains sure should learn from the example of how a shop can sell things that taste home made.

Next week it's the Mighty Accordion and Dancing Shoes Week. My daughter-in-law promised to send my three oldest grandchildren to me on the bus. Because they have the little one, who doesn't sleep very well, and they have the christening to organise.

That's what it's like, at the beginning and end of life. You need a lot of sleep, but for some reason you don't always get it.

I sure won't be telling anyone that this new life is really rather pleasant. When my son and daughter-in-law visit, at first I always mutter that they force me to go to church and then that they could visit more often. You have to keep them on their toes a little.

My son asks me whether I'm still thinking about death. Well, it's like this: you put things in order and then you don't think about them until it's time. These days I'd rather study the community college brochure that dropped through my letterbox. I'm wondering whether I should go on a renovation course. Either as a teacher or a pupil.

One project still remains to be done.

I'm not satisfied with my coffin. It's the wrong size. It was done without enough light; I got the colours completely wrong.

Well, I took the coffin apart and wondered what on earth to do with that good timber, the velvet, the fabric, the decorated nails and hinges.

I'll make a present.

I'll make a cot for my son and daughter-in-law's little person, one which has good sides to clatter. One to sleep in, and spend nothing but happy days.

Meet the Grump

He first ruined his day in a radio monologue in 2009.

It was a typical commission for a Finnish writer. Little time to write, low pay, the use of one actor. The content was to be comic. After a couple of wakeful nights an old man began to speak through me, his comedy arising from his seriousness.

I remember my friend's grandfather well, his day was ruined when the Berlin Wall came down. Grandpa Erkki didn't mind the collapse of socialism, but he didn't like the botched job they were making of it. Why were they tapping away with their little hammers? On a demolition site you need a foreman, storage and a recycling plan. You don't footle about in denim jackets and sneakers. Why do it wrong when you can do it right?

I was also inspired by the opinion columns of small local papers, where I first noticed that nothing is too small to ruin a Finn's day. One day sunshine, the next day rain. From my own grandparents I learned not to waste money on unnecessary things like lemonade. My father-in-law has grown his own potatoes and onions all his life, and a person doesn't need much more than that. In addition to all this, I myself was born into this world at the spiritual age of 82.

I wrote the twenty stories as commissioned, for the mouth of an actor. The impetus for this flood of words from a quiet man came from his doctor's opinion that his veins would clog if he didn't change his diet, reducing his salt and fat intake. But the Grump knew that his veins were clogging because so many things ruined his day. He had to let them out.

The world changes; the Grump does not. This is what drives the story, but it is also true. In Finland the Grump's generation was born, in the sauna, in the 1930s. They grew up during the years of the Second World War, lived through rationing and rebuilt the country. During their lifetime an agrarian country became a technological country. Today the grandson or granddaughter of an illiterate peasant receives a free school and university education. Everyone has a smartphone, with a direct connection to, for example, the President of the United States, when before you had to ski over marsh and lake just to see your neighbour.

As the skills of machines increase, those of people decline. As artificial intelligence grows, people become stupider. The most sophisticated technology in world history is, in the

Grump's opinion, in the hands of the stupidest generation in history. It's a pity that his own descendants are members of precisely that generation.

In the old days, everything was simpler. For the Grump, the first is always best: car, house, wife. Things and attitudes don't necessarily improve.

Being a grump, however, does not depend on age or gender. It's an attitude that is visible even in the furrowed brow of some babies: things were better in the old days.

I myself was born in 1974, and since 1985 everything has been getting, if not worse, then more difficult. Why isn't a VHS player good enough for humankind? Why do we need a DVD player and everything that came afterwards? *Dempsey and Makepeace* is enough; I don't need *Game of Thrones*.

Being a grump isn't nationality dependent either. I have met grumps from Italy, Estonia, Iceland, Ireland, the USA and Great Britain. All human societies have their good old days – most of them their boiled potatoes and the nostalgia for newspapers printed on paper.

Grumps sit in pubs and petrol stations, on park benches and local trains. They write letters to the editor and above all they grumble in their own minds about the ineptitude of young folk. For them, there is only one proper newsreader, for the Finns; Arvi Lind, for the Americans; Walter Cronkite, for the Brits; Richard Baker. The man who, every day at the same time was on the television screen, told the truth the way it is, unsmiling.

But the Grump is not a racist, a nationalist or a bitter old shit. He does not resist progress, but stupidity. But most progress is unnecessary, like air conditioning in cars, talking about feelings, and divorce. You should learn to put up with difficult things. The Grump is a conservative anarchist who always has a suggestion to make about things that ruin his day. He demands that people should view the world with a longer perspective and concentrate less on their own selves.

The Grump does not laugh at himself or at other people.

The readers laughed.

I received more feedback from my radio listeners than from my preceding ten years as a writer. People recognised their grandfather, their grandmother, their uncle; sometimes the Grump stared back at them in the mirror. Some thanked me for finally speaking the truth. Some took the character as satire; others were as irritated as they were irritated by their uncle's comments at family celebrations.

The radio monologues became a book; the book became a play. The Grump had a column in the country's biggest newspaper. Politicians said what ruined their days. Their plagiarism was pathetic, but for the character it was the same as what happened to the Sex Pistols. Any publicity is good publicity.

The Grump movie, directed by Dome Karukoski, had 500,000 viewers, which is ridiculous in a country of five million. It meant that many a local grump had started his car and driven (patiently, to keep his fuel consumption down) to the cinema to watch a story lacking unnecessary violence and sex. They were probably a little bothered by the fact that it had colour. Generally the Grump has reached many readers who do not otherwise read. Fortunately, their wives and mothers read and give them books for their birthday, Christmas and Father's Day. I have been able to take literature to places where it has never before been: sports events, garages, prisons and the hands and minds of teenage boys.

A chance commission grew into an empire. It has sort of ruined my day. The audio books have been awarded three golden discs, which was not my first thought when I began my career as a writer in the wardrobe of my childhood home.

But was everything better in the old days? What is to be found behind that thought?

An increasingly fragile old man whose life is contracting. His wife lies in a health-centre ward, his own health is acting up, his children and his grandchildren visit too seldomly. Technology, customs and food are becoming incomprehensible. Society regards the man as old, an expense item, although in his own mind he is still the forty-two-year-old young man who built his house with his own hands and was responsible for providing for his family.

He is our father, our mother, our grandfather, our grandmother. That is the profundity of the Grump, without which the story would have been a short one. Beneath the crusty surface is a soft person longing for a listener. He wants to convey his skills and his knowledge, to connect with other people, because otherwise this life is pointless. Grumps are not the best at putting things into words, but you have to try to understand meanings. As the Grump says: *Don't listen to what I say, listen to what I mean.*

Now the Grump is going to have a chance to ruin the day of English readers. What would Grandpa Erkki, who has been in his grave for a long time, have thought of this? Probably, it would ruin his day. Why translate books into a foreign language, when they probably haven't even had time to read their own literature?

Happy ruining your day.

Helsinki, 21 July 2017
Tuomas Kyrö

Marc Raabe

Cut

Some men are born evil

A gripping serial killer thriller

THE INTERNATIONAL BESTSELLER

THE CLEANER

ELISABETH HERRMANN

Gisa Klönne

SILENT IS THE FOREST

INGE LÖHNIG

THE WAGES OF SIN

A KIDNAP.
A CRUCIFIXION.
A MURDERER ON THE LOOSE.

THE INTERNATIONAL BESTSELLER

MARTIN KRIST

FIELD OF GIRLS

MANILLA

The best of European crime fiction

www.manillabooks.com

KARL OLSBERG
DELETE

A dangerous game — or
a murderous reality?

HEIDELBERG REQUIEM

Wolfgang Burger

HANNA WINTER

He must hunt her down.
Kill her.
Destroy her . . .

SACRIFICE